SNOOPING CAN BE
Dangerous

LINDA HUDSON HOAGLAND

Linda Hudson Hoagland

LITTLE CREEK BOOKS
A division of Mountain Girl Press
Bristol, VA

LITTLE CREEK BOOKS
A division of Mountain Girl Press
Bristol, VA

This is a work of fiction. Any resemblance to actual persons, either living or dead is entirely coincidental. All names, characters, and events are the product of the author's imagination.

Snooping Can Be Dangerous
Linda Hudson Hoagland

Published June 2012 by Little Creek Books.

ISBN: 978-0-9848050-6-8

You may contact the publisher at:
Little Creek Books
Bristol, VA 24201-3655
Email: publisher@littlecreekbooks.com

Dear Reader,

I have been a long time and proud resident of Southwest Virginia and the Appalachian Mountains in my small Town of Tazewell. I am a retired employee of the Tazewell County Public Schools where I worked as a purchase order clerk for more than twenty years. I have two sons, Mike and Matt, who are wonderful, of course, and a newly acquired (about a year ago) daughter-in-law, Becky.

I have been writing all of my life but I didn't get my first book published until 2006 at my age of 55 and I have been trying to make up for lost time since that date because I waited so very long to get it done.

I would like to welcome you to my world of Lindsay Harris as she tries to get through her life one day at a time with the hopes of reaching old age feeling as though she has accomplished something.

Lindsay is a character partially formed from my years as a legal secretary/assistant and my desire to make the job a little more interesting than the repetitive typing of one legal form after another.

I hope you like Lindsay and her antics as she explores the world that surrounds her to find answers that make sense.

This is the first of a series of mystery stories that will follow Lindsay, her family, and her friends as she tries to outrun all of the trouble and mischief that she blunders into without much effort on her part leading her to the thought that *Snooping Can Be Dangerous*.

Yours truly,

Linda Hudson Hoagland, Author

Acknowledgements

Tammy Robinson Smith, my publisher, has enough faith in me to think that I might be able to start and continue writing a mystery series. Thank you, Tammy, for believing in me and allowing me to do what I love to do.

Sloane Trentham Uphoff, editor, deserves my thanks for putting up with my need to resist change and then telling me it would be better for the manuscript.

Thank you, Joe Tennis, for claiming me as your Aunt Linda and allowing me to share in a friendship that I will always cherish.

Thank you Adda Leah Davis for accepting me as a friend, warts and all.

Thanks to all of my writer friends who share their successes and failures with me and I with them. When we work together, we all become better writers.

Thanks to the Appalachian Authors Guild, Lost State Writers Guild, West Virginia Writers, and Reminiscent Writers for allowing me to be a member and participate in functions that have allowed me to improve my writing skills.

This book is dedicated to the memories of:

Ezra Walter Hudson, my father,

Winifred Ellen Hudson, my mother,

and

Lavern Wilber Hoagland, my husband.

Without them

Linda Hudson Hoagland, Author,

Wouldn't be.

Chapter 1

"Anna?" I said.

"Yes, Ma'am," answered Anna.

"Please don't call me Ma'am. My name is Lindsay or Linds for short."

"Yes, Ma'~err~Linds," said Anna.

"Have you ever worked in a law office?" I asked.

"No, Ma'~Linds, this is my first full-time job. I hope I'll do okay," she answered in a high-pitched, anxiety filled voice.

"You will, Anna. You will be just fine. I'll show you how to answer the telephones correctly and greet the walk-in clients. That's all you will need to do for a while; at least, until you feel comfortable with it. Then you will get into bigger and better things," I said.

A day of training was not what I needed, but that didn't matter. Once again, I was training a new, unsuspecting young lady how to survive the world of Wayne Maxwell, Attorney at Law.

Working in Wayne's world could be and was very trying. Wayne was a prima donna of the law profession. In Wayne's world, the only evident truth was his. The only way to win Wayne's trust and respect was to do everything just as he instructed you to do it.

I couldn't explain that to Anna, not then anyway. I was sure if I told her about the tantrums that Wayne displayed periodically; she wouldn't stay long enough for me to get her trained. That's the way it happened with several previous trainees.

Wayne's employee turnover rate was unparalleled in the town of Richwell. Only the desperate and/or ignorant need apply, which meant that those applying for a job should only do so if there was nothing else available in the county or the applicant was so new into the working world that she was totally unaware of the terror tales of Wayne Maxwell.

I was sure that Anna probably fit into both categories. She was young, fresh out of high school, desperate enough to jump at the first office job offered to her, and she hadn't been out in the job hunting venue long enough to hear or to believe any of the rumors about the heartless Wayne Maxwell.

I, too, was desperate when I was hired by Wayne to do grunt work, but I was old enough to fight back when the occasion would arise. Of course, I had to watch my mouth because I really needed the job and Wayne knew it.

Wayne arrived with a bang of the door and a loud shout.

"Lindsay!"

I cringed at the sound of my name. It was going to be a bad day. His tone of voice told me that.

I hurriedly rose from my seat behind my desk with the tingles of fear running up and down my spine. The fear wasn't for me but for Anna.

"What, Wayne?" I shouted back at him.

"Where is the Smithson file?" he bellowed.

"On your desk," I answered.

I heard him stomping into his office, mumbling to himself.

I entered his office as he reached for the file he needed.

"Wayne, lower your voice a decibel or two. Please don't scare Anna off right now. I need her to answer the phone if you want me to get the Jameson closing ready by this afternoon," I pleaded.

"I'm not trying to scare anybody off, Lindsay. Why would you say that?" he asked in an obvious controlled tone.

As soon as my mouth slammed shut, I knew I had said the wrong thing; namely, the truth.

"Forget it, Wayne. Just go on to your hearing before you're late," I said softly so Anna couldn't hear my words.

"We will discuss this later, Lindsay," said Wayne in a dismissive tone.

"Yes, Sir," I replied in a penitent tone. I knew if I acted sorry, or at least sounded sorry, maybe he would forget about it. Then again, maybe not.

A few moments after Wayne exited the office before I could breathe a sigh of relief, Everett sauntered into the lobby with a beaming smile on his round face.

"Why, hello," he said to Anna.

"Hello to you," replied Anna as she returned his infectious smile.

"I'm Everett. I work here once in a while," he said as he explained his reason for taking up a good deal of space in the small waiting area.

Everett stood well over six feet tall with a girth that displayed the attributes of a well-fed man.

"I'm Anna and this is my first day here," she answered softly.

"Welcome, Anna," he said as he walked down the hall.

I raised my hand in a wave or salute as the giant figure of Everett passed my open office door. Maybe the day wouldn't be so bad now that Everett was here. Everett always had a calming effect on me as he did with Wayne most of the time.

I opened the Jameson file and spread the contents across my desk. I needed to type the deed of trust as well as the deed in its final form for the signature of all parties involved in the transfer of property from seller to buyer. Pretty cut and dried duties bordering a bit on the boring.

My mind wandered to the Smithson file in Wayne's possession. Wayne hadn't told me anything about the contents of the file, but I had heard the rumors and read all of the stories in the newspaper.

"Forget about that file, Lindsay. You've got work to do," I admonished myself in my feeble effort to keep my mind focused on my duties.

Chapter 2

The telephone blared through the house. I always turned the ringer on high on every phone to jar all of us into reality. The phones were plentiful within the confines of our walls. The girls, Ellen and Emily, had one. Ryan had his extension, and there were additional phones in the living room, the kitchen, and, of course, I had one in my bedroom. It kept the fighting down amongst the crowd, but we didn't count on privacy because eavesdropping had become a major pastime.

"Hello," I answered impatiently as I stirred the liquid mixture in the boiling pot on the burner heated to bright red on the left side front of the kitchen range.

"Lindsay, this is Justin," said a stern, authoritative voice.

"What do you want?" I asked dreading the answer.

"Marilyn and I want to take the kids to visit my mother and father in Ohio this weekend. We want to stop in a King's Island for a day for fun. I will pick them up Friday morning and be back Sunday evening," he explained in a flurry of loud words.

"Who is Marilyn?" was all I could think to ask.

"She lives with me. I want to see how the kids get along with her. It is my weekend, you know. Instead of Friday evening, I want to pick them up early that morning. You don't have a problem with that, do you?" he questioned me sternly.

"No, that will be fine. But remember, according to the custody agreement you aren't supposed to take them out of the state."

"They are going to see their grandparents. That is allowed," he said sarcastically.

"Their grandparents are supposed to come here to visit," I countered.

"They are getting old, Lindsay. We are going to see them. It may be the last time we get to see my mother. She hasn't been doing well health wise," he continued to explain impatiently.

"Are you telling me the truth, Justin?" I questioned.

"Of course, Lindsay. Why would I lie to you about that?" This time the tone was condescending.

"Justin, you have spent your life since I've known you lying to me. Why would I believe you now?" I said loudly.

"It's my mother, Lindsay. I want her to see the kids. I want her to see how much they have grown. You know what I mean," he said trying to sound like he was pleading.

"I'll let the kids decide, Justin," I said as I covered the mouthpiece and yelled to my kids, "Pick up the phone Emily, Ellen and Ryan. Your father wants to talk to you."

I continued to listen as I heard the hellos from the loves of my life, my children.

"Hey, Guys, are you all there?" Justin asked.

"Yes," three distinctly different voices chimed in response.

"I'm going to pick you up early, say about seven in the morning so we can go to King's Island. Do you want to go?" he said with excitement.

"Yes, yes, yes . . ." each of my loves responded.

"Lindsay, I know you are still there. You heard them. They want to go, and I will pick them up early Friday. You can have the weekend all to yourself. You can write all those lies you insist on putting in your short stories. That reminds me, how much money do you make from selling those lies?" he asked sarcastically.

"No money, Justin, I donate my stories to a literary magazine. The magazine is a nonprofit and can't afford to pay the contributors. I do get free copies for my writing shelf. For your information, Justin, they are not lies, and they are not all about you."

There was a loud sound, and I was sure Justin had slammed the receiver down on his end of the conversation.

I began to shake all over which was my normal reaction to Justin and his temper.

"Mom, Mom, you're going to let us go, aren't you?" pleaded Emily.

I hesitated before answering. "Yes, you can go."

All three of my children hung up each of their phones, rushed to me, and threw their arms around me and each other as they whispered, "Thank you, Mom, thank you, thank you, thank you . . ."

They were ecstatically happy, and tears were streaming down my cheeks. I was so afraid I made the wrong decision. I brushed the tears from my face quickly so the kids couldn't see the pain.

"If you have any dirty clothes that you want to take with you, bring them to me so I can wash them for you," I instructed my brood with a fake smile plastered on my trembling lips.

My children scrambled in search dirty clothes to pile into the laundry basket. I let the food sit on the stove while they gathered their dirty laundry.

I didn't set the table. There was no need to do that because each of them would ask me if he or she could eat in his or her all important bedroom. Since the family broke up with Justin going his way and me my way, family fellowship had been sorely lacking.

When I thought earlier that morning that it was going to be a bad day, I didn't think I was talking about what was going to be taking place at home.

My work day actually was pleasant with the appearance of Everett and the calming affect he had on Wayne. The court hearing that Wayne had to attend must have gone as he expected, because he didn't appear to be put out by whatever decision was made.

The loan closing that I had prepared for that same afternoon couldn't have been easier. All parties were agreeable, all problems had been settled, and they were more than willing to put an end to the legalities.

So I thought my premonition of a bad day was wrong. I so much wanted my premonition to be wrong. Needless to say, it wasn't and the "wrong" appeared in the form of my ex-husband rearing his ugly head.

While speaking with Justin, I should have mentioned the child support or lack of it, even though I knew I was fighting a losing battle. Occasionally, I liked to remind him that he fathered three beautiful children and that he should contribute monetarily to their successful rise to adulthood.

Oh, well. Maybe I'll mention it the next time. I wasn't up to the fight at that time.

Chapter 3

Wayne wasn't at work the next day. He said he was going to the neighboring county to do some real estate research. I think he was just going to see some of his old law school buddies.

The pressure cooker was set aside for the day, and Anna and I could take care of daily routine business. Besides, I wanted to talk to Everett, if he came in, about Justin and my decision to let the kids go with him. I needed a sounding board. I needed to express my fears aloud. I needed him to tell me I didn't do the wrong thing.

I was day dreaming when I was suddenly jolted to reality.

"Lindsay, you have a call on line one. He said to tell you it's Joe," said a cheerful Anna. She, too, was feeling the lack of pressure with the absence of Wayne. You could hear the relief in her happy voice.

I was not expecting a call from Joe, but I loved talking with him. He made me laugh and forget about my sorry, mixed-up world.

"Hey, Joe, what'cha know?" was my normal greeting to him.

"What's going on with the Smithson case? Wayne Maxwell is the attorney, isn't he?" Joe asked.

"Yes, but I don't know anything about it. Even if I did, I couldn't tell you," I said with obvious irritation.

"I know that, Linds. I'm just aggravating you," he teased.

"You're doing a good job. Aggravating me, I mean," I said sullenly.

"Remember, Lindsay, I write for the newspaper, but I do human interest features, not the blood and guts stuff," he reminded me.

"I know, I know. I'm just trying to stay out of trouble, Joe. That's all. I still love you." That last phrase was said with a great, big, huge smile across my face.

"Love you, too, Linds," he said with the a big smile that I could see in my mind.

"How is the Mrs.?" I asked in order to steer the conversation to something other than the Smithson case.

"She's fine, and the baby is growing like a weed. She should be walking soon. Linds, the real reason I am calling is to invite you to my book signing. I've finally received a case of my book, *Discover Southwest Virginia* from the publisher, and my first book signing will be Friday night at the library. Betty and the baby, Amy, are supposed to be there. We all would like to see you. Bring your kids, too," he said cheerfully.

"I can be there, but my kids won't. I'll tell you about that when I see you. I would truly love to see you and the family," I answered as I, too, tried to be cheerful.

"If you find out any dirt on the Smithson thing tell me then. I'm just curious, Linds. This is not for the newspaper," he assured me.

"I'm curious, too, Joe, but Wayne has not let me see anything related to that file. I have typed some of the everyday motions that are filed in all murder cases, but I have seen nothing related to this murder. Like you, everything I know has come from the newspaper and local news broadcasts. I've heard a lot of speculation. I'll be happy to share that with you," I explained.

"Okay, Linds, I'll see you Friday night," he said as he hurriedly hung up the receiver.

That smile was still plastered across my face when Anna entered my office.

"Lindsay has a boyfriend! Lindsay has a boyfriend," Anna chanted.

"Sorry, Anna. Joe and I are friends. I'm much too old to consider him that way. My relationship with him is that of a sister and her baby brother. He comes to me when he needs to sound off, and I listen. Everyone needs a sounding board. I'm his."

"There are men who really like older women, you know," Anna continued with the teasing.

"I was his boss a few years ago at a volunteer thing we were doing for a local charity. For some reason, we clicked and became fast friends. I have watched his progress through college and his marriage to Betty followed by the birth of Amy. I love him with all my heart, but it's a sister's love."

"Yeah, sure," said Anna in a tone sounding unconvinced.

Chapter 4

"Wayne Maxwell, Attorney at Law," chirped Anna into the telephone receiver as she tried to fulfill her receptionist duties per explicit instruction from me.

"Lindsay Harris, please," said a voice in a whisper.

"May I tell her who is calling?" asked Anna.

"Marnie," whispered the voice.

"One moment, please," Anna said she placed the call on hold.

"Lindsay, someone named Marnie is on line one. You have some interesting sounding friends. They sound much more interesting than the friends of Mr. Maxwell."

"What do you mean?" I asked. I didn't think my friends were particularly interesting.

"Marnie sounds mysterious like she is whispering so no one can hear her other than the person she is calling," explained Anna.

"Well, I guess that's true. Her boss is probably standing within earshot, and she doesn't want him to know she's making a personal phone call. I do the same thing when Wayne is around," I said.

I disconnected Anna and pushed the button to retrieve Marnie's call.

"Hi, Marnie. What's new?" I said.

"Want to meet me for lunch?" whispered Marnie.

"Yeah, sure. Is there a problem?" I asked.

"Nope, just some gossip I want to tell you about," she replied.

"Who is it about?" I asked.

"I can't tell you right now. Meet me at noon at the drugstore," she whispered softer than before.

"Okay, see you there," I said as I hung up the receiver puzzled about the secrecy.

"Oh well, just a couple of hours to wait," I mumbled as I tackled the dreaded Dictaphone and the monotone voice of Wayne telling me word for word what I needed to do on the next boring real estate file.

I turned the Dictaphone off gleefully. It was lunch time, and I was happy to walk away from Wayne's voice even for only an hour. I thanked my lucky stars that he was out of town for the day. The only time he would call in to check on the daily occurrences was at 4:55 p.m. He scheduled it for that precise hour to satisfy himself that I had not had the audacity to leave work early.

People told me he was a deacon in his church and that his wife, Louise, dearly loved him. I found that hard to believe. Maybe he was a completely different man when he was not in the office. No, I didn't think so.

Enough of Wayne. I wanted to think about bigger and better topics. At the top of my thoughts was gossip. Marnie was supposed to tell me some of it. She seemed to have a pipeline to all the tales of the town.

"Hey, Marnie, over here," I said in a voice barely above a whisper as I waved my arms above my head.

"Hey, Linds, did you order yet?" she whispered excitedly.

"No, I was waiting for you," I said as I motioned for the busy server.

Our order was placed hurriedly, so Marnie could start spilling her guts about the gossip that must be burning her tongue.

"Is Wayne defending that guy Smithson?" asked Marnie as she

partially covered her mouth.

"Yes, I think so. To tell you the truth, the only thing I've seen related to that file is the label. That is all he has allowed me to see," I explained.

"Aren't you the person who does all of his motions, et cetera?" asked Marnie.

"Yes, I am, but for some reason he doesn't even want me to touch the Smithson file. I have enough to do without getting into that mess," I said in a tone I used when I tried to convince myself that what I was saying was true.

"Did you make him mad? Doesn't he trust you?" asked Marnie.

"I'm not sure. He did find out that you and I are friends. He wasn't too happy about that, Marnie," I answered.

"Why should that cause any problems?" demanded Marnie.

"It's because you work for the Commonwealth Attorney, Wayne's opponent. He thinks we are comparing notes and that you are telling your boss all of his defense attorney secrets," I explained.

"That's not true," shouted Marnie.

I could see people glancing in our direction.

"Sh-sh-sh Marnie. You are attracting an audience," I cautioned.

Marnie glanced around the room quickly.

"Don't worry about it, Marnie. Just keep your voice down," I whispered.

"Okay, okay, but he is wrong. Anything you and I talk about never gets to my boss through me," Marnie said defensively.

"I know, I know," I whispered.

The server placed our burger platters in front of us and left quickly to attend to another table of impatient diners.

"What's the news?" I asked once we were alone again.

"You remember that trial where the Johnson woman was accused of killing that man in Richwell?" Marnie asked as she furtively glanced around us.

"Yes, it was in the news. She was found guilty of robbing that old man, but she didn't kill him," I answered.

"Well, Smithson was her partner," Marnie added.

"Our Smithson? Wayne's client?" I asked.

"Yes, he's the one," Marnie answered.

"How do you know that? Did you see the Smithson file?" I probed.

"No, I didn't see the Smithson file. I'm a file clerk and the Johnson file was buried in the closed files until yesterday afternoon. I glanced inside the Johnson file just to make sure I had the right one. You know how that is. I didn't want to have to make another trip into the back room because I had the wrong one. Anyway – I saw the Smithson name in there and I put two and two together," she explained hurriedly.

"I didn't know she was involved," I whispered conspiratorially.

"If the Johnson woman didn't kill the old man, and Smithson was her partner, then he had to kill her. Don't you agree, Linds?" asked Marnie.

"You would have to think that. No one else was there. It had to be him," I answered.

"Yeah, that is what I think. How is Wayne going to defend him? How can Wayne defend a man who is so obviously guilty?" asked Marnie.

"It's his job, Marnie. The guy has to have a lawyer. You know that," I said sullenly.

"Job or not, I wouldn't want to defend a killer,"Marnie whispered harshly.

"Maybe he wasn't the killer. Maybe the Johnson woman was, and she had a good lawyer that got her off," I explained.

Marnie looked at her watch and said "I've got to go, Linds. I'm going to be late if I don't leave now."

"Okay, okay, I'm right behind you," I said as I grabbed my handbag and left a tip on the table. "You go on ahead, Marnie. I'll pay the bill. You can pay the next time."

I walked to the cash register with the feeling that I was being watched. I turned quickly to catch the eyes boring into my back.

All present, mostly males sitting at the tables, had their heads down concentrating on the food before each of them

The cashier took my money, and I exited the restaurant trying to escape the sudden dread that overtook my good spirits.

Chapter 5

"Lindsay, Wayne has called four times since you left for lunch," Anna said worriedly.

"What did he want?" I asked.

"He wouldn't tell me," Anna responded.

"Where is he?" I asked.

"On his way here," explained Anna.

"Why?" I asked.

"I don't know. He wouldn't tell me," said Anna.

"Anna, you go on to lunch. Take your time, and don't worry about Wayne," I said as I tried to rush her out of the office before Wayne returned.

"Are you sure. He has a temper on him. Don't you want me to stay?" Anna asked.

"No, no, I'll be just fine. Wayne can scream all he wants. I'm used to it, if you know what I mean," I said.

"I don't see how you can get used to that verbal abuse, Lindsay," stated Anna.

"If I have to work, Wayne knows I have to work, then I have to develop a thick skin and the ability to tune him out or bow down to his superiority. I have done all of those on occasion. I will continue to do what is necessary to appease Wayne as long as I plan to work here," I explained.

"That's not fair to you, Lindsay," said Anna.

"It really doesn't matter, Anna. I would rather it be me than you because I don't want you to leave. Just go on to lunch, take all the time you need. I will be here to cover for you," I said as I tried to get her moving along to lunch.

"Thanks, Linds," Anna said softly.

Anna and Wayne must have passed each other in the parking lot. As soon as the dust settled from Anna's exit, Wayne burst into the lobby aching for a fight.

"Lindsay, where is Anna going?" he demanded.

"To lunch," I replied.

"Isn't it past the lunch hour," he questioned loudly.

"No. What is your problem, Wayne? What can I do to help you?" I asked firmly.

"Someone is giving information to the Commonwealth Attorney's office. Is that someone you, Lindsay?" he demanded.

"How can I do that, Wayne? You won't let me see the file," I said as my voice pitch started to rise.

"There is a reason for that, Lindsay," he snarled.

"Anna hasn't seen the file either, has she?" I asked in a tone matching his.

"If you two aren't talking, how can the information get to him or his office?" he shouted.

"I can't tell you that, Wayne. All the information I have came from the newspaper or word-of-mouth. There are a lot of people talking about your case. It's probably the biggest news story that has ever happened in this town," I said angrily. My anger was forcing the tears to flood my eyes.

Everett walked up behind Wayne. He must have heard the accusations being made. As a matter of fact, I didn't even know he was in the office.

"Wayne, these ladies would not cause you harm knowingly. You need to back off a little, or you're not going to have any employees working for you." These words were issued with a smile plastered across Everett's face.

"Everett, someone is talking," said Wayne in a somewhat quieter tone.

"What about you, Wayne? Who have you been talking to? Someone must have a direct pipeline," questioned Everett.

"I'm not talking to anyone connected with that office," he sputtered.

"I know that. Have you been investigating, checking out your client's story?" asked Everett.

"Of course, I have to do that, Everett," replied Wayne.

"Well, one of your witnesses will probably be a witness for the state," added Everett.

"Yes. I suppose that could be true. The only people I have talked with have been his family members. They said they believe him and support him all the way. Someone's got to be lying to me," said an exasperated Wayne.

Wayne turned and left the lobby where I was working at the moment covering for Anna. He never apologized. He never did apologize, no matter what.

Everett seemed to have settled Wayne for a while, but I could foretell the future and the accusations would fly again. I needed to get Anna ready for the onslaught.

Chapter 6

"Did your father say anything to you guys about being late?" I asked as I glanced at the clock again.

"No, no, no," answered three voices as they, too, looked anxious.

"I'm going to be late for work if he doesn't get here soon," I muttered. "Are you sure you guys have everything you need?" I asked knowing perfectly well that they were all set and ready to go.

Ellen shrugged her shoulder in response. I believed she was the only one listening to me.

Emily and Ryan had begun a shoving match.

"Stop that now," I told them just loud enough to get their attention.

"Where is he, Mom?" asked Emily.

"If you start whining, I'll make you stay home, Emily," I said harshly.

Of course, she glared at me like I was a germ caught under a microscope.

"Get rid of the look, Young Lady," I said firmly.

"Yes, Ma'am," replied a sullen Emily.

What if he doesn't pick them up? I wondered. *They will be so disappointed, and I don't have a baby-sitter for the day.*

I began the pacing of a caged animal, stopping only to glance out the front window checking for the arrival of his car.

I don't even know what kind of car he drives, I thought.

"Mom, didn't dad say he would be here at seven?" asked Ellen as she stared at the clock.

"Yes, but I guess something came up to make him late," I answered as I tried to soothe her worries with a plausible explanation.

"He could have at least called," said an extremely unhappy Emily who was very near tears.

"Don't worry, Guys. He'll be here," I said with all of the encouragement I could muster up.

I knew he had done this to me many times in the past. *Not showing up when we had plans was his way of putting me in my place and punishing me for whatever wrong he thought had occurred,* I mused. *He should not, and I mean NOT, be doing this to his kids.*

Eight o'clock, he still wasn't here, and I was supposed to be at work.

"Anna, this is Lindsay. I'm going to be late. My ex-husband has not arrived yet to pick up the kids. I haven't heard from him, so I don't know what time he will get here. Is Everett there?"

"Yes, but Wayne hasn't come in yet," Anna said.

"Well, tell them both I will be there as soon as I can. Call me if you need something. I am at home waiting," I said trying to hide my frustration.

"Okay, Linds, no problem," said Anna.

I knew Anna would be fine as long as Everett was there to keep Wayne off of her back.

Suddenly the doorbell rang, and all three children raced to grab the door knob.

"Daddy?" Ryan screamed as loud as he could.

"Ryan, shut up!" I shouted above the noise.

"Lindsay, don't yell at him. He is just glad to see me," said a father who had been gone for a very long time.

"I have a headache, Justin. Tell him to shut up, please," I pleaded knowing the words were falling on deaf ears.

Emily and Ellen each grabbled her bag of clothes. Emily punched Ryan in the side and motioned for him to pick up his bag.

"Go to the car, Kids. Say hello to Marilyn. She is going to be with us. I'll be there as soon as I speak with your mother," said Justin.

He turned to me and smiled the same smile that I wanted to smack off of his face since our divorce troubles started.

"What is it, Justin?" I asked.

"The kids are looking good," Justin said,

"I know they are, no thanks to you," I snapped.

The smile twitched but remained intact.

"Why didn't you call to let me know you would be late?" I asked.

"I was kind of busy," he answered in a "jerky" tone.

"Not near a telephone?" I continued.

"As a matter of fact, I wasn't near a telephone," he remarked.

"Then where were you?" I urged.

"If you must know, my car was parked along the side of the road while I changed a flat tire. Once I changed the tire, I drove directly to a tire store to get another one for a spare. They weren't able to repair the one I removed from the car. Are you satisfied?" he asked in a smart-alecky tone.

"Yes, I am. Everyone was worried, that's all. You know how kids get when they have to wait for someone to pick them up," I said sharply.

"No, not really," he replied.

"It's not pleasant," I answered sullenly.

"What else do you need to know?" he demanded.

"Phone number, addresses and anything else I might need to know if an emergency crops up," I said.

"I have it all written down on this card," he said as he handed me an index card.

"You will bring them back late Sunday?"I questioned.

"Yes, Lindsay, I will. I've got to go. We are running late because of the flat tire."

I glanced around the living room to see if anything was forgotten.

"Okay, be careful," I said to Justin as he ran down the front porch steps. I waved to my children, my reason for living, as they rode away in my ex-husband's car.

I was worried. I couldn't really put my finger on a reason, but the worry was there roaming around in my brain interfering with all of my thoughts.

I waited for a few minutes before I tried to get myself together enough to get on the road and drive to work.

I was already two hours late, and I hated to be late. I would rather take the whole day off work than walk in late.

"Wayne, please don't be there when I arrive," I prayed loudly as I drove the twenty miles to work. I lived in Stillwell County, but my home was in Richwell. I promised myself, again, that I was going to move to the town of Stillwell so I wouldn't have to drive so far. That was not likely to happen; at least not until I won a million dollars in the lottery.

Luck wasn't with me this day, which was really obvious from the way the day started. My arrival at the office only accented the fact that I must have had a dark cloud floating over my head.

Wayne was at the office – waiting for me.

As soon as I walked through the door I was warned by a wild-eyed look from Anna.

"He's been looking for you, Lindsay," Anna whispered.

"Well, I'm here now," I said as I hurried passed Anna, hoping to get to my office so I could put my handbag down along with a few other items I carried into the office to snack on and drink.

"Lindsay!" came a shout from Wayne's office at the end of the hall.

I continued to walk to my office and ignore his shout for the moment. I opened my desk drawer and proceeded to put my things where they belonged.

Suddenly Wayne was filling my doorway with his angry, shaking body.

"I'll be in your office in a moment, Wayne. I just needed to unload my arms from the packages I was carrying," I offered in weak explanation.

"Where were you, Lindsay?" he snarled.

"At home, I was waiting for my ex-husband to pick up his children. He was late therefore I am late. I'm very sorry that I have caused you so much distress, Wayne," I said as apologetically as I could muster.

"I need the Baker file," he snapped.

"It's in the file cabinet. Anna could have retrieved it for you. Or you could have found it in the B's without any problem, Wayne," I said trying to control the sarcasm that was tingeing my tone heavily.

"It's not Anna's job to find that file. It's your job, Lindsay. If you don't want to do that job, Lindsay, you can be replaced," he growled.

"Yes, Sir, I'll get the file for you," I said as I tried to stem the tide of angry tears.

I walked rapidly to the doorway and stood toe to toe in front of Wayne.

"Are you planning to move so I can get the file?" I asked in a controlled tone.

Wayne glared at me and side stepped to let me pass.

I located the file exactly where I told him it would be. I placed the file on his desk and walked back to my office where I closed the door and offered a prayer begging for peace.

I had no idea what drove him to be in such an uproar. Truthfully, if I didn't need my job, I wouldn't take all of the abuse.

A gentle tapping on my closed door roused me from my thoughts.

"Come in," I whispered softly.

Everett opened the door slowly.

"Come on in, Everett, and please close the door behind you," I said.

"Lindsay, are you all right?" asked the concerned Everett as he looked at the tear streaks on my face.

"Yes, just mad, that's all," I said as I tried to force myself not to cry anymore. "Please sit, Everett. I need to talk to you."

"Don't worry about what Wayne said, Lindsay. He is just under a lot of scrutiny with the Smithson case," Everett explained.

"I'm not worried about what he said, Everett, at least, no more than I usually am," I said.

"What's the problem?" Everett asked.

"My ex," I said.

"What's happening? You don't talk about him much. I thought he was out of state and out of your life," said Everett.

"So did I, Everett. I think we both assumed wrong," I said solemnly.

"Tell me about it, Lindsay," Everett urged.

"He has my kids right now. He says he taking them to see their ailing grandmother. That part I believe. On the way to his mother's house, he is taking them to an amusement park. He has his current live-in with him, so there will be two of them looking after the three kids," I started.

"You said it was all right for all of this to happen, I guess," he prodded.

"Yes, Sir, I did," I answered.

"What's the problem?" he asked.

"My gut tells me he is not going to bring them back to me on Sunday," I said reluctantly.

"Did he give you any reason to believe that?" asked Everett.

"If you're asking me if he said he wasn't bringing them back, no, he didn't. Quite the contrary. He assured me he would bring them back on Sunday. That's a dead giveaway for me. He is a liar through and through," I explained.

"You know you can't do anything until he doesn't bring them back, don't you?" Everett said.

"Yes, I know. I guess I just needed you to tell me that. I'm so worried. I think I've really made a big mistake by letting him take my children out of state," I said as I choked back the tears.

"Wait until Sunday, Linds. If he doesn't show up with the kids, give me a call at home. Okay?" Everett said encouragingly.

"Yes, Sir," I said still struggling with the tears.

"Now I can see why Wayne's little hissy fit just made you angry. You've got bigger problems to worry about, don't you?" he whispered softly.

I nodded my head in agreement and Everett got up to leave.

"Thanks, Everett, you can leave the door open now. I think I can face the world for a little while longer." I said as I took a deep breath.

Chapter 7

My phone rang and Anna announced, "Joe is on line one."

Good, I thought. *I really needed to talk to an insane person.* Of course, I thought that with a smile on my face.

"Hey, Joe. What'cha know?" I teased.

"Lindsay, I've got some news," Joe answered.

"What about?" I asked.

"You know, the matter we talked about earlier," he continued.

I sifted through my memories and stopped on the Smithson case.

"What's the news?" I asked.

"The prosecution says they have an eyewitness that can prove he did the deed," he explained.

"Who?" I asked.

"My source wouldn't tell me who it is. Do you have any ideas about who it could be?" Joe probed.

"No, none. I haven't ever seen the file," I answered.

"According to the info I have, since his lady partner was not prosecuted for murder, only robbery, and if he didn't do it according to your boss, the old man didn't do it because he died, then who else was there?" he asked.

"No one, Joe. No one else was there according to the lady and the client. If the woman didn't do it, he had to," I said in explanation.

"Yeah, that's what I thought, Linds. Your boss sure can pick them," Joe said showing his sarcasm.

"He didn't pick this one. He was appointed to defend the man by the judge. He could have said no but he thought the publicity might be good for business. I'm beginning to think that was a mistake. My boss is an absolute bear. You can't stand to be around him," I said.

"Maybe you ought to mention to him that there is a rumor about a witness," Joe suggested.

"No, never. He thinks I'm giving the newspapers information as it is. If someone is doing that, it isn't me. The only thing I know is what you tell me," I said defensively.

"I see your problem. Someone needs to let the defense know," urged Joe.

"Not me!" I said with emphasis.

"Are you coming to my book signing tonight?" he asked.

"Yes. I'll be there with bells on to tell everyone what a wonderful writer you are," I teased.

"You don't have to tell anybody that, Linds. I just want you there, okay?" he said.

"Okay, no problem, Joe. Is there anything wrong?" I asked.

"I hope some people show up. It doesn't feel so good if you have a party and no one shows up to help you celebrate," he said in a sulking tone.

"That's not going to happen, Joe," I said softly.

"I wouldn't be so sure about that, Lindsay. Writers lead such a solitary life," he said.

"You don't lead a solitary life. I'm sure you are hardly ever alone," I said.

"Well, that's true. What with my newspaper job, my wife and my daughter, I find it hard to write sometimes," he continued.

"See what I mean?" I asked forcing a lilt to my voice.

"Yeah, gotta go. See you later, Lindsay," he said hurriedly.

I hung up the phone.

Chapter 8

The work day ended without any more verbiage from Wayne about my morning lateness.

I didn't have to rush right home as I normally would do because my children were with their father.

I decided to visit the local consignment shop to see what I could find to wear that was new to me. I loved to buy good clothes at bargain prices, so a consignment shop was right up my alley of fine things to do.

"Lindsay, it's good to see you," shouted Mary across the aisles of clothes when she saw me enter her used clothing store.

"Got anything new?" I asked.

"Sure do. I think there are some things your girls would like right there in front of you. Good prices, too," said Mary.

I looked at the shorts and jeans. Mary wasn't kidding. Name brand jeans for rock bottom prices. I didn't know whether I should buy them or not without my girls trying them on to see if they fit. The girls could be so picky about what they wear. They were not like their mother. I was just learning to be picky.

"Mary, can you hold these behind the counter until I can get my girls in here next week?" I asked.

"Sure, Lindsay, no problem. Why didn't you bring them with you today?" asked Mary.

"They are visiting their father and grandmother. I am footloose and fancy free all weekend," I tried to answer with a happy sound.

"In that case, I have some new stuff in your size, too, in the next aisle over to your right," Mary urged.

"Thanks," I whispered happily as I walked to explore the clothing she pointed out to me.

I had been trying to look more professional in my office appearance. At least, I was trying to look better as long as my pocket book allowed me to do so.

My taste as of late had moved toward nice looking pants and jackets and away from the dress with panty hose routine.

I thought a professional woman looked really good in pants and jackets. To put it more to my way of thinking, a professional woman was a lot more comfortable in pants and jackets.

I pulled a couple of pair of pants and two matching jackets off of the rack. I carried them to Mary and paid her without even trying them on to check the fit. I knew they would be perfect other than maybe being a little too long, but I could fix that no time at all.

"You don't have anything new for a young boy about ten years old, do you?" I asked.

"No, not today," Mary answered.

"I'll see you next week, Mary," I said as I hurried out the door to my car.

I knew I was going to be late to Joe's book signing if I didn't get a move on. It would take me an hour and fifteen minutes to drive to Abingdon to help him share his victory.

I walked into the bookstore to see a table completely surrounded by people, and my mind went back to his thought that no one would show up.

Each member of the crowd was holding a copy of his new book and waiting patiently in line for him to personally sign his or her clutched copy.

I decided to do the same thing, and I grabbed a copy of the book so I, too, could get a personal signature.

"To Lindsay, with love. That's how you need to sign it," I said.

Joe had his head down when I thrust the book into his hands. He looked up to me in total surprise.

"Lindsay, you're here," he said loudly.

"I told you I would be," I answered with a big smile.

"Look at all of these people," he said excitedly. "I had no idea there would be that many here."

"I did, Joe. You write a good newspaper column, so I was sure they would want to see more of what you can do," I told him.

"You have more faith in me than I do," he said softly.

"I always do," I added with a smile. "Where's your wife and daughter?" I asked as I looked around the room.

"Something came up and they couldn't be here. They both send you their best," he said quietly.

"Oh, I'm so sorry they can't share your joy," I said.

"So am I," he countered.

"I'm going to look around a bit after you sign my book. When you get a break we can talk. Okay?" I said.

"Sounds good," said Joe as he was handed another book to sign. I looked behind me and saw several more people lining up for the personalized signature from Joe.

I was hoping to run into someone I knew, but I didn't travel in the same circles of those people with whom I work.

Like Joe, I was also a writer, but most of my writing had not been exposed to those who knew me other than the people in my writing circle of friends. I had let go of a few short stories, and I had been lucky enough to have them published, but most of my writing was for my eyes only at that point in my life. Eventually I would let others see it, but not just then. Too much of it was personal feelings that I didn't want to share.

I was browsing through the books about the art of writing when I was poked in the ribs by a laughing Joe. I was really surprised he didn't tousle my hair on the top of my head which was his normal show of affection.

"Lindsay, the bookstore is almost out of my books. I'm so shocked," he sputtered joyously.

"A star is born!" I shouted so all present in the bookstore could hear.

"Stop that!" he whispered loudly. "Linds, I have some more news for you," he whispered softly so that only he and I could hear the exchange of words. There was no mention of names. It was safer that way.

"What is it?" I asked.

"It's a neighbor," he answered.

"What neighbor?" I probed.

"Don't know. I was told it was a neighbor," he answered.

"Have you ever driven by the house?" I asked.

"No," he said.

"I have. It's actually not too far from where I live. From what I can see, the closest neighbor to the old man was about a half mile down the road. The house is actually a trailer permanently affixed to the ground. He has several out buildings, but all of it is sort of run down and in disrepair," I explained.

"Didn't he have any close neighbors? I wonder why a neighbor would be peering in the door or window of the old man's house?" said Joe as he was musing out loud.

"Don't have a clue, Joe," I said.

"Linds, do you know any of the people around where he lives?" Joe asked.

"I might. I'm not really sure," I answered.

"Can you ask any questions without getting into trouble with Wayne?" Joe asked.

"I should be able to do that. After all, they are my neighbors, too," I said.

"When can you do it?" Joe continued.

"What about tomorrow?" I asked.

"Great, call me if you get any info, okay?" asked Joe.

"What do you really want to know, Joe?" I questioned.

"If there really is a neighbor, who is the witness? Maybe this is just a bluff, a tale that they want to get leaked to Wayne. It makes me think the prosecution doesn't have a very good case," added Joe.

"Joe, it's getting late. I need to get started for home. It will take me longer than an hour and I've got to stop and get something to eat. I'm really hungry," I said.

"Okay, Linds, I'm so glad you came," Joe said.

"I wish your wife and daughter had been here," I added.

"Me, too," he said as he cast his look down to the floor.

The drive was long, and I was tired. Sleeping wouldn't be a problem tonight.

Chapter 9

I had a Saturday spread out in front of me; a free Saturday with no kids telling me to take them here and there. I was lost, totally lost. My life had been kid driven for so long.

I was sipping on a cup of coffee trying to figure out how I was going to drop in on neighbors I hardly knew to do some snooping for Joe.

The telephone startled me back to reality away from my world of musing and wondering. I reached across the kitchen table to grab the noisy instrument.

"Hello," I said harshly.

"Linds, is everything all right?" asked Marnie.

"Oh – Hi, Marnie. Yes, everything is fine. The phone startled me, that's all," I said apologetically.

"I heard you are without kids today. Do you want to go shopping?" Marnie asked.

"Yes. I would love to do that, but I've got to visit a couple of neighbors before I can hit the road," I answered.

"Is there a death?" asked Marnie.

"No, not really. Well, yes, but it happened several months ago," I said.

"What are you talking about, Linds?" asked Marnie.

"Well, you know the topic we were discussing the last time we had lunch, and we both discovered that information was being kept from both of us because we are friends," I explained.

"You mean the Sm ~ " she started to say before I interrupted her.

"Don't say it, Marnie. The walls have ears," I said as I cautioned her against using names.

"What about it?" asked Marnie.

"This whole scenario takes place in my neighborhood, and I've been told that someone else was present when the event occurred," I explained.

"You're kidding?" said Marnie.

"That's what is being said. My girls are friends of one of the girls who is the closest neighbor to where it all took place. I'm going to drop in looking for a ring that one of my daughters has lost. You want to come with me," I asked conspiratorially.

"I sure do. I'll be right over in a jiff. I'll bring some breakfast, too," suggested Marnie.

"Good, I don't want to cook anything. I'll pay you when you get here," I said.

"What do you want?" Marnie asked.

"Surprise me," I answered.

Marnie was true to her word. I was barely dressed before she was knocking at my door.

"I got us both a breakfast platter and some juice," she said as she rushed passed me to the kitchen.

"Thanks," I said as I started removing the papers that surrounded the food.

"Who is it we are going to talk to?" asked Marnie excitedly.

"Mavis Jefferson," I said softly.

"Do you think the place is bugged?" asked a scared Marnie as she glanced around the room.

"I don't know," I said " I'm just afraid to say too much for fear of being accused again of something I haven't done. Except this time, it's different. This time I am going to do it, and you are going to be with me. We've just got to be careful, that's all."

"Yeah, right," said Marnie.

We talked about the people we worked with in the gossipy tone of two teenagers as we ate our breakfast.

"What excuse are you going to use to talk to the people?" asked Marnie.

"I have a real reason. Emily lost her birthstone ring, and she thinks she may have left it at Kate's home. Mavis Jefferson is Kate's mother, so we are going to ask Mavis if she remembers seeing the ring lying around the house. Then, I will go from there," I explained.

"Sounds good because it is legitimate," remarks Marnie.

"Let's go, if you're finished eating," I said.

"Sure, okay. Let me throw the trash in the can," said Marnie.

The trip was short and sweet. We were standing in front of Mavis's door in less than five minutes.

"Mavis," I said to the tall slender lady who answered the door.

"No, I'm Gail. Mavis is my sister."

"You two sure look alike," I said in surprise.

"That's what everyone tells us. I'm actually two years older than Mavis," said Gail.

"Is Mavis home?" I asked,

"Yes," answered Gail.

"May I speak with her? I'm, Lindsay, Ellen's and Emily's mother, and they are friends of Kate. This is Marnie, my friend from work, who is going to go shopping with me."

"Just a moment. I'll get her, but won't you come in first," said Gail.

I looked at Marnie, and we both crossed the threshold into the Jefferson house.

Mavis appeared before us almost magically. She must have been standing to the side watching everything and listening to the exchange of conversation between us and her sister, Gail.

"Hello, Lindsay, what can I do for you?" asked Mavis.

"Mavis, this is Marnie, a coworker of mine. She is traveling with me today. The reason I'm here is to find out if my daughter left her birthstone ring here by any chance," I explained.

"No, I don't believe she did. Kate never mentioned finding a ring.

33

I will ask her when she gets home today. Is there anything else?" asked Mavis in a dismissive tone.

I didn't want this conversation to end as abruptly as Mavis obviously did. I had no other choice, at this point, other than to ask her my question point blank.

"Yes, there is. Do you know anything about the death of the old man that was killed about a half mile from here? It is my understanding that you or a member of your household was a witness to the killing. Is that true?" I asked in a flurry of words.

"I knew you had another reason for appearing at my door. Your daughter probably didn't lose her ring, did she?" asked Mavis.

"Yes, Ma'am, she did. She was too embarrassed to accuse Kate of keeping the ring after she left it here. The question about the murder is because a newspaper friend of mine asked me to find out," I answered as my face turned pink with embarrassment.

"Are you accusing my daughter of stealing the ring?" demanded Mavis.

"No, I'm not; neither is my daughter. All she wants to know is did she leave the ring here?" I asked.

"Like I said earlier, I will ask Kate. As far as seeing the murder is concerned, it wasn't me who saw the old man dying," answered Mavis.

"Who was it? Do you know?" I asked.

"It was my daughter. It was Kate. She hasn't been the same since she saw the old man," said Mavis trying to hide her concern for her daughter.

"Did she see the actual killing?" I probed.

"No, she saw him after he was left for dead. She was walking the dog that we no longer have, and he led her to the old man's house. She peeked in the window and saw the convulsing body. She had nightmares, one right after another. She has missed a lot of school because of what she saw," answered Mavis.

"I'm so sorry to hear that Kate was the one to find him. I never really knew who did. I thought the death had been reported by a man," I said.

"It was. When Kate came home, my husband talked with her and told her not to say a word to anyone about what she saw. He walked to the old man's house, peeked through the window like she did, then he came back and told her he would call the police," said Mavis.

"Was the old man still alive?" I asked.

"No, there was no movement at all. The convulsing must have stopped soon after Kate saw him," answered Mavis.

"Then no one actually saw anything other than a dying or dead body," I said.

"No. She saw no one at the house or leaving the house," added Mavis.

"You don't know of anyone else who could have seen something or someone do you?" I probed.

"No. Only us, and we are sorry any of this has happened; especially Kate," answered Mavis.

"Well, we'll be going, Mavis, but please ask Kate if she has seen the ring here or anywhere else. I'm just about to give up hope for ever finding it," I said trying to convince her that I had a real reason for being there.

"She really did lose her ring?" asked Mavis.

"Yes, she did," I answered while looking directly at her.

Marnie and I walked to the car in silence. We were trying to digest everything we had heard. The words burst forth from both of us as soon as we climbed into the car.

"Do you believe what she was saying?" asked Marnie.

"Not completely," I answered.

"What part don't you believe?" asked Marnie.

"That part about coming home and telling her dad. Oh, I believe she told her father, but I also believe it was long after she saw the convulsing body going through the final throes of death. Another thing: Why didn't Kate call the police and not her father?" I said.

"What do you think happened, Lindsay?" asked Marnie.

"I'll have to think about it. From what I have gathered from the newspapers and such, the old man's body was cold and decomposing when he was found and hauled off to the medical examiner in Roanoke," I said.

"How long do you think he had been dead?" asked Marnie.

"At least two or three days is what I read," I answered.

"Are you going to tell Wayne what you found?" asked Marnie.

"No way. You're not going to tell your boss, are you?" I asked.

"Can't. He would probably fire me," Marnie answered.

"I guess I'll tell Joe. He is the one who actually sent me on the snooping trip," I said,

The shopping trip proved to be a let down after all of the talk of the morning with Mavis. Neither of us was in the mood to window shop.

Marnie and I both needed to think about what we should do.

Chapter 10

It was Sunday morning, and I was up and out of bed way too early. I decided to skip church since my children were gone, but maybe I should have gone anyway so the day would pass much faster.

The inspiration wasn't there. I didn't go to church, and I knew I was going to be burned in the eternal fires for missing the Sunday sermon.

I tried to busy myself with small jobs that I had put off doing forever and a day. My mind kept telling me it's busy work, and my constant glances at the clock were not helping.

I picked up the telephone and started dialing a number. I placed the receiver back on the hook before I have entered all of the digits.

I picked up the receiver again, dialed the complete number and listened to the ringing at the other end of the phone line.

"Hello," said a bored sounding voice.

"Marnie, what are you doing today?" I asked.

"Nothing in particular, why?" she responded.

"Come over here, and we'll watch a rented movie and eat some popcorn," I suggested.

"I should be cleaning the house," said Marnie.

"Me, too, but I didn't want to do that. I've got to hang around here all day waiting for my kids to get home. I thought I might call Joe while you're here, so we both can talk to him about what was said by Mavis. How about it?" I asked.

"Okay. Do you want me to pick up a movie?" Marnie said.

"Yes, please," I replied.

Marnie was at my door in less than an hour with the newest George Clooney movie clutched to her chest.

"Should we watch the movie first or call Joe first?" I asked knowing she was going to choose the movie.

"I'll pop the corn in the microwave. You can come keep me company if you want," I said.

"You and Joe. What is that?" Marnie asked.

"There is no me and Joe. He is a friend. I'm old enough, almost, to be his mother. I think of myself as his big sister. We are friends and, hopefully, we will always be friends," I explained.

"Oh, okay. You just seem to talk about him a lot. Just asking," said Marnie.

"No problem. He actually is like a baby brother to me, and I want to keep it that way," I added.

"What have you got to wash down the popcorn?" asked Marnie.

"Diet Cokes," I said.

"Good. I'll get us one," Marnie said as she opened the refrigerator. "Who are you planning to feed all of this food to?"

"I couldn't sleep last night, so I made some of the favorites for my kids to eat when they get home later today. I miss them so much," I said.

"I guess you do," said Marnie as she gazed at the covered bowls stacked on the refrigerator shelves.

"Let's go put the movie in the VCR," I said.

We sat and passed away two hours of movie that engrossed us both to the point that we had to pause the flick any time we had to take a bathroom break.

Late afternoon arrived. Marnie and I were playing cards to keep ourselves entertained.

"Do you want to call Joe now?" asked Marnie. "I need to be going home soon to get some work done at the house."

I gathered up the cards, stuffing them back into the box before I went in search of my small telephone book containing all of the phone numbers important to me.

"Okay, I've got it," I said .

I grabbed the phone in the kitchen and started dialing Joe's number. After eight noisy rings without an answer, I placed the receiver onto the base.

"No answer, Marnie. He and his wife must be out and about. I'll try again tomorrow," I said as I walked back into the living room where Marnie had been sitting next to the extension. She was awaiting the shout from me to pick up the extension so we both could talk to Joe at the same time.

"In that case, Linds, I'm going to go home. When are your kids supposed to come home?" asked Marnie.

"My ex said late today. I don't know how late though," I said.

"I'll call you later and check on you, Linds. You're going to be a nervous wreck waiting for them to return," Marnie said as she walked out the front door.

The silence was deafening. My home without my children was something I hadn't endured for a very long time. All three kids were rarely gone from the house at the same time, unless they were with me. Of course, they went to school every day when it was in session, but I went to work, too, so I wasn't home during the quiet part of the day.

I wandered around the house straightening, adjusting, dusting and re-arranging the small items until I had nothing left I could do unless I delved into the big projects.

The light was fading, and I was switching on lamps and glancing out the front windows in search of headlights coming into my driveway.

It was nine o'clock and they were not home. My mind harkened back to the television commercial that asks "Do you know where your children are?" Of course, my answer was a loud, forceful "NO."

The telephone rang.

"Hello? Justin?" I said.

"No, this is Marnie, Lindsay. I take it the kids aren't home yet."

"No, and I'm getting worried, Marnie," I said anxiously.

"Maybe he had car trouble," suggested Marnie.

"Yes, maybe. He was late picking them up because he had a flat tire. Maybe that's all it is. He did say he would be late, but I didn't think it would be this late," I said trying to accept the weak explanation.

"Linds, do you want me to come over and stay with you until he gets there?" asked Marnie.

"No, no. I'm sure they will get here any minute. Thanks, Marnie," I answered.

"Do you want me to call you later? Say in about an hour?" asked Marnie.

"No. Hopefully we will be getting ready for bed by then. I do have to work tomorrow," I said.

"I'll talk to you tomorrow, Linds. Call me if you need me," said Marnie.

"Okay," I said.

My nerves were tingling. I knew he was not going to bring them back to me.

"Dear God. I've made a really big mistake," I prayed as tears rolled down my cheeks.

Chapter 11

I looked for the card with all of the contact telephone numbers for Justin. It was taped to the front of my refrigerator. I yanked it loose from its strips of transparent tape and raced to the living room where I could continue to watch for headlights and the return of my babies.

"Hello," whispered a sleep-filled voice.

"Trula, this is Lindsay. What time did Justin leave your house today?" I asked.

"Lindsay? Lindsay who?" said a confused voice.

"Your former daughter-in-law. That Lindsay. Remember me?" I said as I held tight rein on my temper.

"Why are you calling this hour of the night, Lindsay?" asked Trula sternly.

"Justin is the reason. I'm looking for Justin, Trula. What time did he leave your home today?" I sputtered.

"He didn't," she said with apparent irritation.

"Is he still there?" I pleaded.

"No. I haven't seen Justin for months," Trula said harshly.

"He told me you were very sick, so he was taking the kids to visit you for possibly the last time," I explained.

"I haven't been sick. Anyway, I haven't seen him or spoken with him since he took up with that woman he is running around with," Trula said with disgust.

"You mean, Marilyn?" I asked

"Yes, that woman. I heard she is a slut," said Trula.

"Do you know where Justin is, Trula?" I pleaded.

"No. Now I'm going to hang up and go back to sleep, Lindsay," said Trula.

"Yes, Ma'am," I replied to the woman who always managed to intimidate me.

The sobs of anger spewed forth from my soul. I was angry with Justin, my kids for wanting to go with him and myself for allowing it all to happen.

"What am I supposed to do now?" I asked the surrounding walls that seemed to be closing in on me.

I took deep breath. I needed to get control of my voice, so I could talk again without breaking down completely into uncontrollable sobs.

Another deep breath, and I thought I could do it.

There were two more different numbers listed on that card.

I dialed the first one and it rang and rang and rang. No one picked it up, so I disconnected the line feeling frustrated and angry.

Anger made tears.

"Settle down, Lindsay," I told myself as I forced the tears to stop.

I dialed the next telephone number, the last one that he listed on the card.

Eight, nine, ten rings and no answer.

I slammed down the phone.

It was now midnight, and my kids were not home.

I switched on every light inside and outside of the house. I opened my front door so I could see any on-coming traffic, and I planted myself in the recliner opposite the front door where I intended to stay as I waited for my kids to come home.

My eyelids were heavy, but I was fighting to stay awake. I needed to watch for the headlights. I needed to welcome Ellen, Emily and Ryan into my open arms.

My mind was picturing the greeting I would give them while I smiled and relaxed.

I was asleep.

The telephone rang and startled me awake out of my happy homecoming dream.

"Hello," I said apprehensively into the telephone. It was two o'clock in the morning, and I was trying to shake the sleep fuzzies from my brain as I looked around me and realized that I was in the living room in the recliner with all of the lights ablaze.

"Lindsay, this is Justin," said a cocky-toned voice.

"Are you all right? Are the kids all right? Where are you? Why aren't you here?" I asked one question after another not allowing him to answer.

"Are you finished?" growled Justin.

"Where are my kids?" I demanded.

"With me, and they are staying with me. Marilyn and I intend to keep them, and you will never see them again," he said belligerently.

"Why?" was all I could think of to say.

"They need a good, stable home, and Marilyn and I intend to give them one," he boasted.

Chapter 12

At two in the morning, I knew there was nothing I could do to Justin to get my babies back home.

I showered and got myself ready for work. I ate what I could choke down for breakfast and drank a pot of coffee before I left the house at seven o'clock to drive to work.

I walked through the office door an hour early and headed directly for my tiny office. I needed to get away from the house and the silence of absent children so I could think of what I could do.

Everett was who I needed to see.

Wayne would only cross examine me and tell me how stupid I was for allowing Justin to take the kids in the first place. I didn't need to be told that. I knew how stupid I was when I made that decision. Wayne was without compassion for any of his employees.

Everett would at least try to see my side of the explanation. He would tell me where I went wrong, but he would not make me want to crawl in a hole and die for making the wrong decision.

While I was waiting for Everett to show up, I decided to glance at the newspaper I picked up outside the door where it had been placed by the paper boy.

On the front page at the lower right hand corner was an article about the Smithson case. Of course, I would read it. It wasn't written by Joe, so I released a sigh of relief. Not that Joe wouldn't or couldn't do a good job. He certainly would, but I needed to know he wasn't writing about any of our conversations.

The headlines were:

SMITH TRIAL DATE SET

Wayne was going to be an absolute bear to work with because the trial date was coming up really fast. It seemed to me that it was being rushed through the court system faster than most murder trials.

That was just another problem to stack on top of the one concerning my missing kids.

The rest of the newspaper contained nothing of interest to me. I folded it back into order and took it to the office of the receptionist so others could peruse the pages.

The clock was ticking its way to eight o'clock. That was when people started showing up, usually meaning me and Anna. The lawyers didn't make an appearance until the nine o'clock hour.

"Everett, please come in today," I prayed softly.

I heard Anna bursting through the front door shouting my name.

"I'm here, Anna," I said loudly.

"What are you doing here so early?" she yelled back at me.

"When you get a chance, come in here and I'll tell you," I shouted back at her, not wanting to leave my cocoon of comfort and safety in my office.

Anna hurried herself with making a pot of coffee and appeared in my office in no time at all.

"What gives?" she asked excitedly. "You look terrible. How long have you been here?"

"My ex has stolen my kids, and he said he is not bringing them back home. He said that I would never see them again," I explained as I struggled with tears, again.

"What?" said Anna as her mouth dropped open in total surprise.

"I need to talk to Everett. Is he coming into the office today?" I asked.

"Yes, as far as I know. Do you know where your ex is with the kids?" she questioned me.

"I think they are at his home in Pennsylvania. At least, that's where I hope he is. I wouldn't know where to look for him if he isn't there," I answered.

"What can you do about it if he is not in the state where you live, meaning Virginia?" questioned Marnie.

"I don't know. That's why I need to talk with Everett," I answered as I burst into tears.

Anna did her best to try to console me, but the tears weren't going to stop until I could gain control of myself. That was a very hard task to accomplish.

The sound of the front door opened and closed causing Anna to scurry off to see who had entered the building.

A few moments passed while I tried to dry up the tears before Anna led Everett into my office.

I jumped up from my chair behind my desk and threw my arms around him in a big hug.

"What's this all about?" Everett sputtered with embarrassment.

"I'm just so glad to see you, Everett, because I need your help. It's not advice this time. I really need your help," I said as I released him from his embarrassment.

Anna heard the door open again and took off running to greet the newcomer.

"What has happened, Lindsay?" asked a concerned Everett.

"He has stolen my kids," I said as I struggled to control my emotions.

"Your ex didn't bring them home?" asked Everett.

"No, Sir, he didn't. He called me at two o'clock this morning saying he wasn't bringing them home and that I would never see them again," I explained.

"Do you have your divorce and custody papers available?" asked Everett.

"No. They are at home. I never thought about your having to see them," I said with a shake of my head.

"That's okay, Lindsay. Bring them to me tomorrow. In the meantime, try not to worry. I can't do anything until I have those papers. Your divorce was local, wasn't it?" Everett probed.

"No, I was living in Ohio at the time," I answered.

"Well, that makes it a little more difficult, but I will do what I can. Where is he living now?" continued Everett with questions.

"In Pennsylvania," I answered.

"Another state heard from," muttered Everett.

"Is there going to be a problem?" I asked half scared out of my mind.

"Only with time, Lindsay. Bring me those papers first thing tomorrow morning. I will spend my day clearing my calendar and boning up on the law where it concerns out of state divorces and custody proclamations," said Everett in a consoling tone.

"I'm so sorry to drop all of this on you, Everett. How much is this going to cost me?" I asked.

"Only the court fees. Don't worry about paying me, Lindsay. You are family," said Everett softly.

"Are you going to tell Wayne?" I asked.

"I will have to do it unless you tell him first, which I think you should do," said Everett.

"I was afraid you would say that," I said as I stared at the floor.

"You will tell him, won't you, Lindsay?" asked Everett.

"Yes, Sir, as soon as I get a chance," I said reluctantly.

The chance came immediately after Everett left my office.

"Lindsay," shouted Wayne from his office.

"Coming," I answered back to his annoying shout. Why he couldn't use the intercom was beyond me.

"I need you to do the Jones real estate deed and deed of trust today. I am going to do the title search this morning, but the bank wants to close this deal as soon as possible," Wayne barked his commands.

"Yes, Sir. Wayne?" I said.

"What is it?" he snapped.

His responding tone made me cringe.

"I need to talk to you about a personal problem," I said softly.

"Can't it wait?" he asked.

"It won't take long," I added.

"Well?" he said.

"My ex-husband has stolen my children, and Everett is going to help me get them back," I said in a flurry of run-on words.

"Slower, Lindsay. I didn't understand you. You're talking too fast," he admonished.

I struggled with the lump in my throat. I gazed at the floor as I started speaking again.

"My ex-husband, Justin, supposedly took my children to see their dying grandmother, which I found out was a total and complete lie, and he called me to say that he was never bringing them back to me. He said I would never see them again," I said as I tried hard not to cry.

Wayne looked at me as if I were a piece of dirt that he would like to flick away from his desk.

"Why did you let him take your kids?" he asked with a smirk.

"To see their dying grandmother. I never dreamed that tale was a lie. I did call his mother, their grandmother, and she told me she wasn't sick nor was she dying; at least, not yet. He had not been to see her at any time this past weekend. She said she hadn't seen him for months; not since he started running around with Marilyn. She is his wife, I think. Justin's mother doesn't like her at all. I don't know Marilyn. I saw her sitting in the car when they picked up the kids," I explained.

"What do you want me to do, Lindsay?" Wayne asked.

"Nothing, Wayne. Everett said he would help me," I answered.

"Good, good. I'm so busy with the Smithson matter," said Wayne in his dismissive tone of voice.

I walked out of his office in a daze. Why couldn't he at least show a little bit of compassion? He didn't treat his clients this badly. Why did he do this to his employees?

Chapter 13

I walked back to my office feeling relieved because the conversation with Wayne was over and done with.

I needed to get the Jones file ready, but I couldn't do all of it until he did the title search and gave me the information that needed to be printed onto the deed and deed of trust. I hope it wasn't one of those long real estate descriptions filled with numbers.

I decided to type everything I could that didn't require the verbiage to be entered for the deed.

"Lindsay," said a softly speaking Anna.

"Yes?" I answered.

"Joe is on line one," Anna whispered.

"Thanks, Anna," I said as I tried to offer a smile.

Anna knew it was a personal call, so she was trying to keep her voice low to be heard by only me.

I knew it was a personal call, and I really didn't care who else might know that little tidbit of information. I had bigger worries than a personal phone call.

"Hello," I said in a croak as I felt myself tearing up again.

"Hi, Lindsay. Is everything all right? You don't sound right," said a concerned Joe.

How he got that much knowledge from a simple hello was something that went beyond my comprehension.

"No," I answered as I tried to maintain control of my voice and my tears.

"What's wrong? What happened?" Joe asked.

"My kids are gone. My ex-husband stole them," I whispered hoarsely.

"I thought they were visiting their grandmother," stated Joe.

"They were supposed to do that. That's what Justin told me, but I called his mother, and they were never there," I explained.

"Where is he?" probed Joe.

"I guess he is in Pennsylvania. That's where he lives now with his roommate, Marilyn. I don't even know if she is married to him or not," I said as I struggled to maintain control of my emotions.

"What are you going to do?" Joe asked.

"Everett is going to help me get them back," I said.

"How long will that take?" Joe asked.

"I don't know but there are laws from three different states involved," I said.

"I'm so sorry, Lindsay," Joe commiserated.

"Changing the subject, Joe. I tried to call you before all of this happened on Sunday," I said still struggling with my emotions.

"I took Betty and Amy out for the afternoon. Family day for me because I work so much as does my wife," he said.

"I found out some news for you," I said.

"You did? What is it?" asked an excited Joe.

"There is no actual witness, but two different people saw the body before the cops arrived," I stated.

"Who are they?" he asked.

"Kate, a teenager, and her father, Jim. They only saw the aftermath. According to Mavis, Jim's wife and Kate's mother, Kate saw the body when she peeked in the window during the walking of her dog. She told her father. He told Kate to keep her mouth shut. Jim walked to the old man's house, using the back way through the trees like Kate did. He saw the body. He came back to his house and told Kate he would call the police," I related the story to Joe.

"That sounds strange," mused Joe.

"Yes, I agree. Also, I don't think the police were called right away," I said.

"Why do you say that?" Joe asked.

"Well, the paper said the body was in an advanced state of decomposition. Kate told her father when she saw the old man he was convulsing which means he probably was in the last minutes of his life. How could the body have decomposed so much in a day's time?" I asked.

"Makes you wonder, doesn't it?" said Joe as he pondered her thoughts. "Did you tell Wayne all of this?"

"No," I answered.

"Are you going to tell him?" Joe asked.

"I don't know. He has never let me even see the file since all of this started. He was so ugly with me when I told him about my missing kids. I will have to think about that answer, Joe," I said.

"Let me know what you plan to do, Lindsay, about everything, and that includes getting your kids back from the ex," said Joe.

"My mind is a little muddled right now. Do you want me to do anything else for you? Anymore snooping?" I asked.

"No. You don't need the worry right now. I'll call you tomorrow to see how things are going," he said.

"Bye, Joe," I said softly as I struggled with the tears again.

The rest of the day moved slowly with the second, minutes and hours lasting forever.

I wanted to go home and find Justin's telephone number so I could call him and check on the kids. His phone number wasn't on the list he left with me, but I thought I might have it somewhere on another piece of paper in the house. If not, I would call information, or I would call his mother if I had to. I would find it one way or another.

Wayne returned from the courthouse when he had done the real estate title search.

I completed all of the remaining documents for the loan closing for the bank. Finally, I drove home.

Now, the mad search was on. I had to find that telephone number.

Chapter 14

I was running around inside my house looking in every nook and cranny searching for a piece of paper with a telephone number written on it. That piece of paper might not exist because I may have thrown it out in a fit of rage after speaking with Justin for one reason or another.

I searched my handbag, the junk drawer, the box of bills, the box of important papers, my bedroom and the drawers in each of the children's rooms.

I couldn't find it. Where could I have put it? Did I throw it in the trash?

I picked up the telephone and dialed the operator.

"I need information for Torrance, Pennsylvania," I said slowly and clearly.

"One moment, please," said a professional sounding voice. "The area code is 321, and the information phone number is 555-1212."

"Thank you," I said as I rapidly disconnected the line.

I dialed information and it was answered promptly.

"I need the phone number for Justin Harris, please," I said.

"One moment," a pause and then a recording that recited, "There is no listing for that name."

I replaced the receiver.

Maybe the number was in Marilyn's name and not Justin's. Maybe his number was unlisted.

I called his mother.

"Trula, this is Lindsay," I said excitedly.

"What do you want now?" she said angrily.

"I need Justin's telephone number," I snapped.

"What for?" she demanded.

"I need to call him about my kids," I said.

"They are his kids, too," she said harshly.

"Yes, Ma'am, but he never cared about them until now. Please give me his phone number," I said as I forced myself to speak civilly.

She knew how to push my buttons. She always had been able to do that.

"He has stolen my kids. He says he is never going to bring them back to me. He says he is never going to let me see them again. I need that phone number, Trula," I said sternly.

"What are you going to do, Lindsay?" Trula asked.

"First, I'm going to call him. If that doesn't work, my second step will be to drive to Pennsylvania to kill him. Do you understand me, Trula? When I kill him, you will have to raise my children. Do you want to do that?" I screamed into the telephone.

"Lindsay, please don't do anything stupid," she pleaded.

"He should have thought of that when he stole my kids. I want my kids back. He has done nothing to support them. The only reason I allowed him to take them is that he lied to me telling me you were dying. Now, are you going to give me that phone number?" I asked firmly.

"I'll get it. Hang on until I get my address book," Trula said as the laid the phone down on a table.

"I want his address, too. I have one written down here, but I'm not sure it's correct," I lied as I tried to finagle the information from Trula.

Trula returned to the telephone and read me the phone number as well as his address.

"Thanks, Trula. I'll let you know what happens," I said.

"Don't do anything you will regret," she said sternly.

I dialed the phone number she gave me and reached a telephone answer machine reciting the recorded message.

"Hello. This is Justin and Marilyn. Please leave a message at the beep," said the machine.

"Well, it's the right number," I mumbled as I hung up the receiver without leaving a message. "I'll try again later."

My mind was spinning. What could I do?

The papers! I had to find the papers that Everett needed to get everything started legally.

I knew where they were. I just had to retrieve them and place them next to my handbag so I wouldn't forget them the next morning.

My phone rang and I lunged at it thinking it had to be Justin.

"Hello," I said breathlessly into the receiver.

"Lindsay?" questioned a voice.

"Oh, hi, Marnie," I said.

"Is everything all right. What time did your kids get home?" Marnie continued.

"They didn't," I said.

"Tell me what has happened," she demanded.

I went through the whole rigmarole, relating everything to her that I knew and understood.

"Everett's going to help you legally?" she asked.

"Yes," I said trying to choke back my emotions.

"Good. He is the best for the job. Everybody tells me what a good attorney he is," Marnie said with assurance.

"I talked to Joe, Marnie. I told him everything we found out on our snoop excursion," I said changing the subject.

"What did he think?" she asked.

"He didn't say much except to tell me not to do anything else," I answered.

"What else can you do?" asked Marnie.

"I was thinking about taking a walk the same way they were supposed to have traveled to determine for myself what they could see or not see," I said.

"When are you going to do that?" Marnie asked.

"It's too late and too dark now. I'll have to wait until after work tomorrow. Want to come with me?" I asked.

"I sure do," she said excitedly.

Chapter 15

I walked into the office with my papers clutched in my hands to be delivered to Everett. Anna was waiting for everyone as she sat behind her desk recepting the world.

"Hi, Linds. How are you doing?" Anna asked.

"I'm okay, but it sure was a long night of fitful sleep. I didn't hear anything from Justin or the kids, so I hope the kids are muddling through this ordeal without any permanent damage, but I truly think that is doubtful," I answered,

"Has Everett given you any idea of what he plans to do and how long it will take?" said Anna.

"No, he's waiting for these papers I'm holding in my hand so he can determine his next step," I told her.

"Everett should be here soon, Linds," Anna said.

"I know. I'm afraid he is going to tell me it will take months to get this through court," I said.

I walked to my office, placed my handbag on my desk and moved on to the kitchen area to get a cup of coffee.

Anna entered the kitchen in pursuit of the same liquid eye-opener in the form of strong coffee.

"Linds, is there anything I can do to help?" asked Anna.

"I don't think so. Thank you so much for asking Anna," I said with a forced smile.

Anna left the room, and I wanted to cry again. The tears were for the thoughtfulness from a coworker who hardly knew me.

I hurried back to my office to pull out the files I needed to work on that day.

Wayne burst into the office, slamming the door, huffing and stomping back to his office.

I cringed when I heard his footfalls passing my office door.

"Thank you, God," I whispered when he continued walking passed my office door.

"Linds, you have a call on line two," shouted Anna's voice from the intercom. I reached over to touch the volume control turning the shout down a bit, then I picked up the telephone receiver.

"This is Lindsay, may I help you?" I said in a professional voice.

"Mom, can you come get us," whispered a sob-husky voice.

"Ryan? Is that you?" I asked.

"Please, Mom, come and get us," Ryan continued.

"Hang the phone up right now," shouted a voice from the background.

"Ryan!" I shouted into silence.

Anna came running into my office to ask why I was shouting.

"That phone call, Anna! Did you know that was my son?" I asked.

"No, he didn't say he was. He asked for Linds so I thought it might be a personal call. I had no idea it was your son," she sputtered in explanation.

"He didn't say anything to you did he about where he was?" I asked.

"No, he just asked for you. That's all," she said in an apologetic tone.

"Okay, Anna. I'm not upset with you. I'm just trying to find out anything I can about where he is. I think he is in Pennsylvania at the home of his father and Marilyn, who may or may not be his wife," I explained.

"I wish I could tell you more, Linds," said Anna.

"Don't worry about it, Anna. You didn't know," I said as I tried to console her.

"Lindsay!" shouted Wayne.

"Oh, God! Now I have to put up with Wayne and his temper tantrums," I mumbled as I jumped up from my desk chair, grabbed my legal pad and headed towards Wayne's office.

"Lindsay!" he shouted louder.

"I'm on my way, Wayne," I shouted in response.

The moment I entered his office, I knew I was in for another talking to.

"I heard that you have been talking to a newspaper reporter," he said in an accusing tone.

"Who might that be?" I asked.

"You know who I'm talking about," he snarled.

"No, Sir, you need to give me a name, and you need to tell me who told you," I said calmly.

"Do you deny talking to a newspaper reporter?" he demanded,

"I have talked to friends, Wayne," was my vague answer.

"One of those friends is a newspaper reporter. Am I right?" he asked.

"My friend, Joe is a feature writer for the newspaper. He does not write about crime," I said in explanation.

"He is a newspaper reporter, is he not?" he continued to demand.

"Yes," I said.

"You will not talk to him anymore," Wayne instructed.

"You can't tell me that, Wayne. If it's about the Smithson case, remember that you won't even let me see the file. If you have a leak, you will have to look for someone else to blame," I said angrily. "This is the second time you have accused me. There won't be a third time, Wayne. I mean it!"

I walked back to my office, not stomping my feet, not slamming the door, not losing it entirely. How I managed to maintain that much control was a wonder to me. All I wanted to do was to tell him to take his job and shove it as the old song stated. But I didn't. I would be able to do that someday, but, for now, I needed my paycheck.

Everett must have heard the exchange of accusatory words because he called my extension as soon as I returned to my office.

"Yes, Everett, what can I do for you?" I asked politely when he identified himself.

"Come to my office, Lindsay. I need your papers, and I need to talk with you," he said.

"Yes, Sir," I answered.

On my way to Everett's office, I stuck my head into Anna's office to tell her where I would be. I never had to tell her when I was summoned to Wayne's office. The shouts from him always notified her of my movements.

"Lindsay, are you okay?" asked Everett.

"As well as can be expected what with my kids being stolen and Wayne's temper tantrums," I answered sarcastically.

"We will get started on getting your family back today. It may take a while to get it through the courts, but you will get them back legally," he reassured me.

"What can I do about Wayne? He keeps accusing me of telling others about the Smithson case. You heard what he said to me, didn't you?" I asked Everett.

"Yes," he answered solemnly.

"The only thing I know is information I have gathered from the street. I would like to tell him about what I have heard, but that would only make matters worse. What should I do about him, Everett?" I continued.

"He is not just picking on you, Linds. He is always like this when he is in the middle of an important case," said Everett.

"Yes, Sir, but doesn't he know that that is why he has such an enormous turnover of personnel? People just don't want to take that kind of abuse. I'm one of those people," I said firmly.

"I understand why you feel that way, but hang in there, Lindsay. We need to get your kids back before you do anything," he said.

"I know," I replied.

"What kind of information have you gathered from the street, and who is the newspaper reporter he keeps bringing up in your conversations?" Everett asked.

"May I close your office door?" I asked before I proceeded with the answers to his question.

"Sure," he replied.

"Joe Bristol is the newspaper reporter. I've known him since he was in college. I always think of him as my younger brother. We met many years ago working as volunteers for a charity function. He is a feature writer for the newspaper, not a crime writer. He writes about what is fun and good about people. I'm not afraid to tell him anything because he won't print it in the newspaper," I explained.

"Somebody is leaking information, Lindsay. Could he be getting it from you and telling the crime reporter?" he asked.

"No, Sir. You heard me tell Wayne that I've never seen the file. I have heard none of his phone conversations about the case because he always closes his door. He doesn't bring any witnesses or similar sources in here. He always meets them outside of the office. What is there that I can leak? Besides, maybe they are just second guessing him. Maybe they have dealt with him enough to be able to predict what his next move is," I said.

"You're right, Lindsay. If you know anything, it didn't come from this office. You might also be right about the second guessing. Wayne is pretty predictable," he agreed.

"My friend, Marnie works in the commonwealth attorney's office, but she is as clueless as I am. We have compared notes, but she, too, only knows what she hears outside of her office," I said.

"Why were you comparing notes?" he asked.

"Wayne accused me of talking to others, so I wanted to see if she was getting the same kind of treatment from her boss. She was and is, but I sincerely hope her boss isn't acting as badly as Wayne," I said.

"What is the information you've been hearing outside on the streets?" Everett asked.

"All I'm going to say is that it is about a witness. Word on the street is there is one. I know for a fact there isn't one," I said.

"How would you know that, Linds?" Everett asked.

"I did some checking. You can tell Wayne what I've said about the witness, but don't tell him who told you. Promise me," I said to Everett.

"Promise. Now, go on back to work so I can get started on the court filings I need to do to get your family back home," he instructed.

"Yes, Sir," I said as I flashed a weak smile.

Chapter 16

Everett was working on the court papers to be filed to get my kids home again.

Wayne was holed up in his office working on the Smithson case. He seemed to be easing up a bit on the abuse, but that could change with a snap of his fingers.

Anna was doing her level best to make everyone in the office happy.

I was plugging along, waiting for the personal problems to slow down to a crawl.

I was grateful that I was busy with the real estate portion of Wayne's practice. The work kept my mind filled with tasks, forcing me to push aside the worries; at least for a little while.

The worries piled onto my shoulders along with the weight of the world when I went home and was all alone.

I entered my empty house after a workday that ended uneventful. This was the day that, if Wayne had pushed one more of my buttons, job or no job, paycheck or no paycheck, I would have hit the road. I'm sure he guessed that much. That was probably why I heard no more out of him.

The silence in my house was creepy. I was looking in every room and in every closet for something; the ghosts of my children, maybe. I didn't have any idea why I felt I must check every place where someone could hide.

After I completed my search, and while there was still some daylight left, I called Marnie.

"Can you come over and take a walk with me?" I asked, hoping she would say yes.

"Are you going the tree route?" she asked excitedly.

"Sure am. I would like a little company if you're available. Do you have a baseball bat?" I asked.

"Why?" Marnie asked.

"It makes a good weapon for defense purposes," I explained.

"Oh, yeah, okay. I have one. It used to belong to my brother. I keep it by the front door for unwanted visitors," she explained with a laugh.

"I'll get one of Ryan's from his room, and we'll both be ready for trouble," I said.

"Be there in a few," said Marnie.

"Hurry, Marnie. We need to do this before it gets dark," I said.

"Okay. I'm on my way," Marnie said.

She appeared at my front door in less than ten minutes carrying a big heavy wooden bat.

I grabbed Ryan's aluminum bat and a flashlight, just in case, and we walked out my back door moving toward the trees.

We were chattering about the events of the day, paying no attention to our surroundings, until I realized we had actually walked passed the house I was looking for in the dusky evening.

"Oops! We need to turn around, Marnie. We've actually missed the house," I said with a nervous laugh.

"How far back?" she asked warily.

"Not very far. It should be right over there," I said pointing to a dark wooden structure.

We walked slowly through the back yard with tall uncut grass and junk having been tossed to the wayside over the years of habitation in the poorly kept up structure.

When I pointed a finger toward the house, I notice a window that appeared more lit up than the other window a few feet from it. I assumed it was the glint of the setting sun that was shining back at me.

After further thought, I wasn't so sure.

Instead of a glint, there was a light; not a bright light, but a light never the less.

"Look at that," I whispered excitedly to Marnie.

"Look at what?" Marnie asked in a frightened tone.

"The light in that window," I answered.

"It looks like a night light to me," said Marnie. "It's so dim you can hardly notice it."

"Why would a night light be burning? No one has lived here for months," I said.

"Maybe the old man left it on and no one bothered to turn it off," Marnie said. "

"Wouldn't it have burned out weeks ago?" I asked.

"You would think so. Let's take a closer look," Marnie said as she marched head-on toward the dimly lit window,

The window was up off of the ground by a few feet. It was just high enough so that neither of us could see into it, even if we stood on our tiptoes.

"I've got to find something to climb on," said Marnie as she glanced around looking for something that would be strong enough to hold her weight.

"There is an old wooden barrel over there. I'll get that," Marnie said as she walked away from the window.

"Make sure it's sturdy enough for you to stand on without collapsing," I admonished.

"Are you trying to say that I'm fat?" Marnie asked accusingly.

"No, Marnie. I'm saying that this stuff has been outside in the weather for a long time. I wouldn't trust any of it to hold up under extra weight. You aren't fat, Marnie. As my daddy used to say to me, you are pleasingly plump," I said with a giggle.

Marnie pulled on the barrel and then let out an ear-splitting scream.

"Marnie, what's wrong?" I asked.

"A snake just crawled out from under there," she said as she let go of the barrel.

"We'll find something else to climb on, but I don't think it's important now," I said.

"Why?" she asked.

"The light is gone," I said.

"Me and my snake must have scared whoever it is away. Didn't do much good for my nerves either to tell you the truth," explained Marnie as she kicked at the tall grass looking for the snake. "There's an old ladder against the wall on this side of the house. I'll get it, and we can still take a look."

"Okay," I answered in a disappointed tone. I really did want to see where the light came from inside the house. I wanted to know where it disappeared to and with whom.

Before Marnie could drag the ladder to the window, I walked to the back of the house and reached for the door knob. The back door was standing slightly ajar.

"Marnie?" I said.

"What?" replied Marnie.

"The door is open," I said quietly.

"Wait for me," she whispered.

Marnie was standing directly behind me when I shoved the door ever so slightly. It moved with the creaking sound of rusty hinges, and we stepped up into the kitchen of the old man's house.

"Maybe we shouldn't be doing this," said Marnie in a harsh whisper.

"You're probably right. Do you want to turn around and get out of here?" I asked,

"No," she answered. "Do you?"

"No," I replied.

We stepped further inside the kitchen. Both of us were holding our eyes wide open so we would not miss anything that might have jumped out at us.

The floor creaked, but we continued on with another step and then another until we cleared the door completely.

I was leaning forward. Marnie was touching my back following my every movement.

I heard a noise, but before I could turn around, I fell forward. Marnie was falling on top of me.

"Get up, Marnie. Get off of me so I can get up," I whispered.

"Okay, okay, I'm trying," she complained.

"What happened?" I asked.

"Something or someone pushed me," she said as she struggled to rise from the dirty floor.

"Did you see who it was?" I asked.

"No, I was pushed forward on top of you. I think whoever it was ran out the back door behind us while we were struggling on the dirty floor. He or she must have been standing behind the opened door," Marnie said.

"Yes, I guess so," I said softly.

"Who do you think it was?" Marnie asked.

"Probably the killer," I said in a tone of dejection.

"Let's look through the rooms really quick and then get out of here. It's getting too dark to see much," said Marnie.

We saw the white chalk outline on the floor of the living room. I was sure there were blood stains but the falling darkness prevented us from seeing the marks.

"Marnie?" I said.

"Yes," Marnie answered.

"Did the shove feel manly and strong or short and adequate from a female?" I asked.

"I don't know," said Marnie with a shrug of her shoulders.

"Just thought you might have a guess as to male or female," I said softly.

"I just felt the push, and down I went on top of you. I can't even begin to guess the gender of the push," Marnie said.

"Okay, no problem," I said as we exited the through the back door. I closed it as I walked away and heard the lock snap into place.

"He or she must have had a key," I said as we hurried through the yard toward the trees.

"Why do you say that?" asked Marnie as she gasped for breath from the fast walking.

"The door locked when I pulled it closed. Whoever was in there must have unlocked it with a key and set it to relock when we left," I explained.

"Who would have a key?" she asked.

"A trusted neighbor," I answered.

We finished the walk/run back to my house in the dark with our path marked by the glowing flashlight I held in my shaking hand. We kept the conversation to a minimum so we wouldn't waste any breath getting to our destination.

"Look, Marnie," I said as I pointed to my kitchen window. "I didn't leave any lights on in the house when we left because it was still daylight, and I didn't think we would be gone until dark. Now, there is a light on at the back door and in the kitchen window. Someone's been in there," I said.

"Maybe you should call the police," Marnie said with fear etching her tone.

We stood at the edge of my back yard staring at the lighted world just beyond us.

I was looking for movement of any kind. There wasn't any; no shadows, nothing.

"My visitor must be gone," I said softly. "Let's check it out."

"Aren't you going to call the police?" questioned Marnie.

"And tell them what? I may have left those lights blazing when I left. I'm sure I didn't, but that's probably what they will tell me," I said.

"Okay, let's just forge ahead and get ourselves killed," said Marnie in a voice dripping with sarcasm.

"Stay out here if you don't want to come with me. I'll check it out myself," I snapped back at her.

"Let's go. Like you said, he or she is probably gone," Marnie said.

I pulled the key to the back door from my pocket and jabbed it into the lock. I was not trying to be quiet. If anyone who was unwelcome was inside my house, I wanted them to hear me so he, she or they could clear out before I got inside.

"Shouldn't you be trying to be quiet?" asked Marnie.

"No, why should I? This is my house. I don't have to enter quietly," I answered smugly.

"You're just as scared as I am," countered Marnie.

I shrugged my shoulders and pushed my way inside the kitchen banging the door against the wall just to make sure there was no one hiding behind it.

We saw no disturbances or disarray.

Maybe I did leave the lights on when I left.

"Come on into the living room, Marnie. I'm going to try to call my ex. I want to know how my kids are doing," I said loudly.

"Are you sure you want me to stay? That's going to be a very personal conversation," Marnie asked.

"Please stay, Marnie. I may need a witness or a friend to hold me up, if you know what I mean," I said.

I wanted to speak with my kids, but I couldn't abide the thought of having to talk with Justin.

"Marnie, do you want something to drink and a snack?" I asked.

"Yeah, what do you have?" she said.

"Diet Coke and Cheetos. I love those things; the hard ones I mean. I don't like the puffed up ones that turn into dough in your mouth," I said.

"Good description, but I just want the drink," said Marnie.

I got us both a glass filled with ice and Diet Coke. I sat down next to the telephone table.

"Since I want you to be a witness, I will go into the bedroom and place the call. When it is ringing, pick up your extension, cover the mouthpiece with your hand and listen," I instructed.

"Sure, if that's what you want," Marnie agreed.

I dialed Justin's telephone number and waited while it rang a couple of times.

"You can pick up now," I shouted from the bedroom.

The ringing continued.

"I am not hanging up," I mumbled. "Please answer this phone call."

Fifteen – sixteen – seventeen rings.

"Hello," said a breathless voice.

"Justin, this is Lindsay," I said.

"Where did you get this number?" he demanded.

"How are my kids? Can I speak with them?" I said changing the subject abruptly. I didn't want to tell him his mother gave me the phone number.

"Your kids are brats, but my kids are beginning to shape up," he said in a bragging tone.

"What do you mean by that?" I asked.

"I've just about got them whipped into shape. They are beginning to accept the fact that you are dead to them," he bragged.

"Can I speak with each of them?" I begged.

"No, you are dead," he said abruptly.

"Please, Justin. I just want to hear their voices. I want to know that they are all right.," I pleaded.

"No," and the line was silent.

I sat on my bed holding the receiver in my hand and cried.

Marnie was hovering over me trying to console me.

"I'll be okay, Marnie," I said after a few moments of tears. "Go on home. Call me tomorrow, okay?"

She reluctantly left me alone in the silence.

Chapter 17

Again, I lived through another fitful night full of nightmares and very little sleep.

I was robot-like while performing my duties. I knew it took time to get my babies back home, especially if I used the court systems to do it correctly. The waiting wore on my mind and the worry burdened my heart and soul.

"Lindsay, line one, please," Anna said over the intercom.

"Hello," I said absently.

"Lindsay, this is Joe."

I could feel myself smiling inside with those few spoken words.

"Hey, Joe," I responded.

"What's happening?" Joe asked.

"I don't have my kids home yet. Everett is working on the problems and he isn't able to give me a date. All I can do it wait," I explained.

"Have you talked to them?" Joe asked.

"Ryan called here at work one day, but Justin made him hang up the phone. Ryan was crying and begging to come home, and I couldn't help him," I said.

"Have you talked to your ex?" Joe asked.

"He is brainwashing them, Joe. He is trying to make them forget about me and that I ever existed," I said as I tried to handle my emotions.

"They will never, ever forget you, Lindsay. Don't even think that," said Joe.

I couldn't speak for a few moments. I was not sure if it was because of unbearable sadness or anger that was building up inside of me.

"Lindsay, are you there?" asked Joe.

"Yes," I struggled to say. "I'm still here. Just couldn't speak for a moment. Let me take a deep breath, and I'll tell you some more news."

"Wait, maybe I should call you later when you get home," Joe suggested.

"I can tell you now. There is nobody here to hear me," I said.

"No, Lindsay. I'll call you later. Don't tell anything to anybody about our 'thing' until you are out of the office. Don't use your office phones, please," he instructed.

"Okay, I won't," I said with a great deal of confusion muddling my mind.

"What time do you get home, Linds?" Joe asked.

"I should be there at 5:30 p.m. barring any delays here," I replied.

"I'll meet you at your house, Linds. I really have to see you face to face," said Joe.

"What's the matter?" I asked.

"Just watching out for you. Tell your friend to be there, too. I need to let her in on this," said Joe.

"You mean the one who has been with me during my recent visitations?" I asked.

"Yes," was his one word reply.

"I'll call her and tell her to meet me at home at the same time. Okay?" I asked.

"Yes, gotta go. See you later," he said as the line went silent.

He was scaring me. I didn't know if that was his intention or not, but I was down right scared. *What have I gotten myself into?* I thought. *What have I gotten Marnie into?*

I picked up the receiver and dialed Marnie's work number.

"Can you come to my house right after work, say about 5:30 p.m.?" I asked.

"Why?" was her automatic response.

"Joe says it's important," I said.

"Why?" asked Marnie.

"I don't know. He wanted me to get you there so he can talk with both of us," I explained.

"Okay, 5:30 p.m. it is. I have to go. The boss is coming this way," Marnie said as she hung up on me.

My mind didn't feel like it could hold another worry, but there was one waiting for me without a doubt.

I watched for Everett to walk past my door. I needed to tell him about Justin's attempt at brainwashing my kids.

"Everett," I said loud enough for only him to hear.

"Yes, Lindsay," he answered as he entered my office in response.

"I spoke with Justin last evening. He is trying to make my kids forget I ever existed. I'm sure he is mistreating them. What can I do?" I asked.

"Wait. That's all I can tell you. I have filed court motions here in Virginia because this is your place of residence. Papers have also been filed in Pennsylvania, because that is where he has taken them. I am waiting to hear from a lawyer friend in Ohio. I don't think we have to do any filings there, but he will let me know because that is where your divorce and custody were settled. I'm in a waiting mode, and that's all I can tell you for right now," Everett sounded as flustered as I was.

"I understand, but I wanted to let you know what he said. Thanks so much for everything," I gushed at him meaning every word of what I was saying.

The afternoon dragged on and on.

At five o'clock, I was at the door ready to leave, no matter what.

Chapter 18

I approached my house with caution. I really didn't know what was waiting for me.

"Darn that Joe," I mumbled. "He has made me so paranoid."

I saw an old Pontiac that I knew belonged to Joe, and Marnie's Ford was parked in my driveway. I pulled my vehicle into the front yard and now it looked like I was having a party.

"I hope we all enjoy ourselves," I muttered sarcastically.

Neither Joe nor Marnie exited each car when I did. They weren't seated in the front seats of their cars.

"That's strange," I said aloud.

I looked around, and I didn't see them anywhere.

The whole scenario was making me nervous.

I started to push my key into the front door lock when the door suddenly opened.

I saw my three stolen children standing in front of me smiling from ear to ear.

Screams of "mom" and "I love you" filled the air. Tears of pure joy were streaming down my face, and I hugged them to me.

I looked around me. There was no Joe or Marnie standing off to the side. They were not here. Only their cars were in my life at the moment.

"What happened? Why are you here?" I asked Ellen who tended to be the most serious minded member of my brood.

"He got tired of us. He said you have spoiled us so badly that he isn't able to do anything with us no matter how hard he tries," she said with a beaming smile.

"You've got to tell me all about it later, Ellen. Okay?" I said.

She nodded her head and went racing to her room to call a friend.

"Ryan, when you called me and your father made you hang up the phone, what happened next?" I asked.

"Nothing much. He told me never to do that again or we all would be punished, not just me," he said.

"What did he do to punish you guys?" I asked.

"Sometimes he would hit us, but most of the time we didn't get to eat whatever the next meal was," Ryan said.

"Did you watch television?" I asked.

"No," he replied.

"What did you do for fun?" I asked.

"We didn't have any fun. We worked. We cleaned house, took care of the yard, washed clothes and whatever else he and Marilyn didn't want to do," Ryan answered.

"I'm so sorry this happened to you, Ryan. I'm sure glad you're back home," I said as I hugged him again.

Emily had been watching us without saying a word. When Ryan moved on to his bedroom, Emily spoke to me.

"Mom, why is dad so mad at you?" she asked.

"He didn't want me to get a divorce. His mouth said he loved me, but his actions proved otherwise. When I found out that he slept with my best friend, I wanted rid of him. He proved to me then that he didn't truly know what love meant. Does that explain it to you?" I said softly.

"I guess," she said as she, too, walked away to her bedroom. She stopped in mid-step and asked, "Do you still love him, Mom?"

"No, Emily, I don't love him. I don't hate him either. He is your father, so I want to keep the communication channels open for the sake of you, Ellen, and Ryan. I want you to choose whether you want to love him or not. It is entirely up to the three of you, because you have that blood tie to him, and I don't," I said.

She nodded her head and continued on her way with a smile on her face.

All three of my children had vanished from the living room choosing to go to their bedrooms to play, read or whatever. I was standing alone in the living room, looking out of my front door at the cars parked on my driveway. Nowhere to be seen were Joe and Marnie.

Where could they be?

Chapter 19

I let a few minutes pass before I rounded up my brood to go exploring with me. Too many strange things had been happening in my life, and I didn't think I should leave them alone in the house.

"Hey, guys," I said after gathering them all in the living room. "Do you know where the people are that belong to those vehicles parked on the driveway?"

"No," was the in-unison reply I received.

"Well, then, I need you each to get something you can carry with you that you can swing and hit somebody with if they are trying to harm you," I told my children.

"Why, Mom?" asked Ryan, the ever curious one.

"You remember when that old man died that lives down the road from here?" I said.

"Yeah, he was a grouchy old man. He wouldn't let any of us near his yard. If we lost a ball in there, he kept it. He wouldn't give anything back to us," said Ryan.

"Someone killed that old man, Ryan. The person who killed the old man doesn't want anyone to know who he is, so he is trying to scare me away from finding out the truth," I tried to explain so a ten year old would understand me.

"Why?" asked Ryan with the girls looking on curiously.

"There is a man sitting in jail right now that has been accused of hitting the old man over the head and killing him," I said.

"He didn't do it, huh?" said Ryan.

"No, he didn't, and I am pretty sure I know who did. My friends, Joe and Marnie have been helping me figure out this puzzle, and now they are gone; missing from my life, just like you guys were when your father wouldn't bring you back home to me," I said.

"Are we going to look for your friends?" asked Ryan with eyes glinting with excitement.

"Yes, we are," I answered.

"When?" Ryan asked.

"Now. I have one of your bats, Ryan. You get the other one. Emily, Ellen, get something you can carry and use to defend yourself, okay?" I told my children.

They all took off running in search of a defensive weapon. Ryan returned with his other baseball bat, since I had one to carry myself. Emily was carrying a long handle shovel, and Ellen was carrying a hoe that they retrieved from the garage.

I locked all of the doors and windows, and we all marched out of the front door hauling our weapons of defense positioned against our shoulders with the business end of each weapon pointing into the air.

I was leading my little parade up the side of the road in the general direction of the old man's house.

It was a walk of not quite a mile, but the kids were really into the whole scene, with the idea that they were helping me.

I threw my hand up to halt the progress when I saw the house I was seeking materialize before me.

"I want you guys to stay behind me at all times," I explained with all the seriousness I could muster. "Joe and Marnie might be in real trouble, and we will be, too, if we are not careful."

Three sets of wide eyes were staring at me. If someone would have jumped out of the bushes and yelled "BOO!" they would have taken off running, weapons in hand or not. I wasn't so sure that I wouldn't be right behind them, pushing them to run a little faster.

"Get your weapons ready, Guys. Make sure you don't hit each other. Be ready to swing if necessary," I said.

I opened the front gate to the fenced in yard that would take me to his front door over a cracked and creviced sidewalk that was in a severe state of disrepair.

When I arrived at the front door, I knocked loudly, knowing full well that no one lived there; not since the old man was killed. Of course there was no answer to my knock, so I tried to turn the door knob. I had lucked out once before and gotten inside through an unlocked, opened door. I was hoping to do that again.

No such luck. The lock was definitely set, and we would not be allowed entrance through the front door.

"Sh-sh-sh," I said as I held my index finger up in front of my mouth.

I strained to hear any noises that might be coming from inside the house.

"Do you hear anything from in there?" I asked knowing that their hearing was probably much keener than mine because of their youth.

They each shook their heads indicating no sounds.

"Let's go around back," I whispered and I led them on to a different destination. "Be as quiet as you can."

We trooped down off the front porch, around the left side of the house, headed to the back yard. The grass was tall, so I tried to knock it over as I blazed a trail for them to follow me.

"Wait here while I check the back door," I whispered to my child followers.

I walked across the small back porch and quietly turned the knob.

"It's locked," I whispered.

I climbed down from the back porch, and as I did so I heard a noise coming from the right side of the back yard, possibly from the old, dilapidated, storage building that was padlocked.

"Sh-sh-sh," I whispered again.

I crept over to the building where I thought I heard the noise. I positioned my left ear against the wooden outside wall that had been grayed with age. I heard a scratching sound, and when I looked down toward my feet, I saw the biggest gray rat I had ever seen.

I didn't scream, but it took everything within me to contain the desire. I stepped away with a shiver of disgust.

"Nothing. I don't hear a thing. Must have been that big old rat I heard earlier. We may as well go back home," I told my children. "Keep your weapons on your shoulders, but be aware of your surroundings. Let's go."

I led them toward the trees, out of the old man's back yard and away from the unknown danger.

We followed the roadway to the old man's house, and now we were taking the back path to get home. To my way of thinking, making the circle was the best way to look for signs dropped along the way by my missing friends.

"Watch the trees. You don't want you to bang into the limbs with your weapons," I admonished them as we started moving back to our house.

"Mom, there is something shiny over there," said Ellen.

The dusk was beginning to extinguish the evening light, so I didn't see anything where Ellen was pointing. I moved closer to the area.

"A little bit further, Mom. You're almost there. Stop! It's right by you left foot," whispered Ellen.

I bent down and picked up a watch. It was Marnie's wrist watch.

She and Joe must have come this way to go to the old man's house. But why didn't they wait for me to get home?

"Emily, what time did you guys get home?" I asked.

"About five o'clock," Emily replied.

"Were the cars parked on the driveway when your father left you here?" I asked.

"No. Our father pulled onto the driveway and unloaded our stuff," Emily answered.

"Did you get the key from the flower box to get inside the house?" I asked.

Emily nodded her head.

"Your father just drove off and left you?" I asked.

"Yes. He knew you would be home soon from work, and he didn't want to see you, he said," Emily explained.

"Oh. Did you see the cars that are parked on the driveway pull in?" I continued.

"No, I guess we were putting our stuff away in our bedrooms," Emily responded.

"Joe and Marnie didn't ring the doorbell?" I asked.

"No, Mom. They didn't knock either," added Ryan.

I looked around me, and then I realized where I was. I was behind the house where Mavis and Kate lived. There was a mister in the family, but I couldn't remember his name. I really didn't remember ever seeing him with my own eyes.

"Emily, Ellen, have either one of you ever met or seen, with your own eyes, Kate's father?"

"Kate is more Emily's friend than she is mine. I have never seen Kate's father. I actually thought her mother was divorced because he was never around when I've been there, which isn't very often," said Ellen as she nodded to Emily to speak.

"No, I've never seen him either," said Emily in agreement with Ellen. "Kate always told me he was at work if I asked about him. She said his name is Jim. I never thought about it much because we don't have a father in our house."

"Does Kate have an older brother, or an uncle, or a friend of her mother's living in the house?" I asked.

"I don't know, except there have been signs of a man living there. Aftershave lotion, the toilet seat left up, occasionally a piece of male clothing; not much, but there have been a few signs," added Emily.

"We need to stop in and see Kate, don't we, girls?" I said with enthusiasm.

"Sure," responded Ellen as she shook her head in confusion.

"Bring your weapons with you, but lean them against the house when we get to the door," I said as I instructed my troops.

I climbed the steps to the back porch motioning for them to stay on the ground.

I knocked on the back door. We were neighbors, so that shouldn't seem so unusual. I waited a few moments then knocked again, except I pounded a bit louder.

No one answered the door, but I could hear activity from the other side.

I knocked again.

No answer. No more activity could be heard.

"I know there are people inside. I don't know why they won't answer the door," I whispered to them as I remained standing in front of the door.

Suddenly the door opened, and I was pulled inside. My children were standing on the ground with their mouths gaping open as they watched my body being pulled inside the house and the door slamming shut behind me.

Because the kids were on the ground and not on the back porch with me, the occupants of the house must have thought I was alone.

I kicked and tried to scream, but strong, muscular arms surrounded me. The body snatcher's left arm snaked up the side of my body, allowing his hand to cover my mouth.

I was struggling with my feet trying to kick him, but my aim was not good because I was trying to kick backwards without being able to see what I was aiming at.

While I was struggling trying to break the grip of the person holding me, I heard a window shatter, then another, and another, until every window within the weapon-extended reach of my children was broken.

I heard sirens, and the man gripping me loosened up a bit.

"What is happening?" he yelled.

"We are being rescued," I said with a nervous laugh.

I saw Joe and Marnie tied up on chairs in the kitchen where I was standing. The fright seemed to be draining from their eyes.

"Who is out here? Who broke all of the windows?" he screamed.

I calmly answered, "Two thirteen-year-old twin girls and a very brave ten-year-old boy."

"Who are you?" I snapped.

"I'm, Jim, Kate's father. I've seen you pick up your girls from the school. The old man was my rich uncle who is now dead."

"Why haven't you been around?" I asked only because I could.

"Prison. I just got out a few months ago," he answered as he struggled to maintain his hold on me.

"You killed him? You killed your uncle?" I asked,

"What's it to you, Lady?" he snarled.

"Why?" I asked.

"He wouldn't give me any money. The old codger had plenty. I know he did but I couldn't find it and he wouldn't tell me where he hid it," Jim said.

"Why did you grab my friends?" I asked.

"They saw me and started asking questions. I pulled my gun and led them to my wife's home so I could take care of business," he spat out the words.

Suddenly the front door crashed opened, and the town police swarmed into the small kitchen like bees being drawn to honey. All movement stopped when they saw the gun next to my head.

I was afraid to breathe. This frightened man with a gun may not have felt that he had anything to lose, but I did.

I had three wonderful children who had been trying to save the lives of Joe, Marnie, and me, not to mention Mavis and Kate.

"Where are they?" I asked quietly so as not to rile him up any more than he was already.

"Who?" he asked.

"Mavis and Kate," I said softly.

"In the bathroom off the master bedroom," Jim answered.

"Dead?" I asked.

"No, Lady, they are my wife and daughter. I'm not going to kill them. I have them locked away until I can get out of here," he answered.

'Thank God," I whispered. I was so glad to know that they had nothing to do with this.

"Put the gun down! Put the gun down, now!" shouted one the town policemen who was standing in front of us.

"You had better do as he says," I whispered. "He is too close to miss."

He jerked his arm and pushed the gun against the side of my face.

"If he shoots me, I shoot you," he snarled.

"Are you sure you will have enough time to do that?" I asked

Again, he pushed the gun harder against the side of my face.

The policeman in front of us didn't waiver. His gun was pointed directly at the man and, of course, me.

"He's not going to shoot as long as I'm holding you as a shield," he sputtered.

"If I'm going to die, it doesn't matter who kills me, does it? You or the cop?" I asked.

This question must have hit home.

"Okay, okay," Jim said.

"Put the gun on the floor, and kick it out of the way," commanded the policeman.

He did as he was told and was immediately thrown to the floor where he was handcuffed. The policeman jerked him up and led him out of the house to the waiting police car.

Out of the corner of the room, hidden from my sight, came my three children followed by Joe and Marnie. Hugs were to be had by all.

"Joe, what was it you wanted to tell me and Marnie?" I asked.

"I figured out who the killer was," he said sheepishly, "And I was so wrong."

I looked and Joe and Marnie and whispered, "Snooping can be dangerous."

About the Author

Linda Hudson Hoagland of Tazewell, Virginia, graduate of Southwest Virginia Community College, has won acclaim for her novels, short stories, essays, and poems. Many of her works have been published in anthologies such as Cup of Comfort along with the publication of her five mystery novels and six nonfiction books.

A few of the awards won by Linda Hudson Hoagland are as follows:

- 2011 – Women's Memoirs – All Things Labor – Honorable Mention – Penance
- 2011 – Alabama Writers Conclave – Honorable Mention – First Chapter of a Novel – Writing the Circuit
- 2011 – Alabama Writers Conclave – Second Prize – Juvenile Fiction – The Lady in the Sun
- 2011 – Appalachian Heritage Writers Symposium – Second Place – Adult Essay – Surprise Package
- 2011 – Writers-Editors Network International Writing Competition – Honorable Mention – Nonfiction – Getting Myself Primed
- 2011 – Tennessee Mountain Writers – Third Place – Writing for Young People – I Dare You
- 2010 – The Jesse Stuart Prize for Young Adult Writing – Second Place – How's That For Real
- 2010 – Tampa Writers Alliance – Novel – Honorable Mention – Quilt Pieces
- 2010 – Alabama Writers Conclave – Nonfiction – Third Prize – Four Large Eggs
- 2008 – Nominee Governor's Award for the Arts
- 2007 – Sherwood Anderson Short Story Contest – First Place – Category V

Many other awards have not been listed.

Mountain Girl Press

*Fiction that celebrates
the wit, humor and
strength of
Appalachian women*

**Find us on Facebook
at
www.facebook.com/
MountainGirlPress**

www.mountaingirlpress.com

LITTLE CREEK BOOKS
BRISTOL, VIRGINIA

Books for discerning readers

**Find us on Facebook at
www.facebook.com/LittleCreekBooks**

www.littlecreekbooks.com

CPSIA information can be obtained
at www.ICGtesting.com
Printed in the USA
JSHW020801010620
5983JS00002B/118